RESCUED HEART

A COMBAT HEARTS SERIES / TITAN WORLD NOVEL

TARINA DEATON

RESCUED HEART

Combat Hearts Series
A Titan World Novel

Tarina Deaton

To Team Titan.
Thanks for trusting me with your boys.

INTRODUCTION FROM CRISTIN HARBER

Dear Readers,

Welcome to the Titan World books with stories ranging from military romance to paranormal to contemporary romance. There's something for everyone—action-packed romance, swoon-worthy moments, and happily ever after!

When I started the Titan series, I wanted to combine my love of steamy romance and action-packed suspense. I wrote strong men and women that I hoped readers would fall in love with. I can't think of anything more exciting than opening my world up to very talented authors to extend that experience so that you, the reader, can have a deeper connection to more than one book series at a time.

You will meet new characters and see them interact with familiar ones; you will also see the interpretation of the Titan universe through another author's eyes. I hope that you take the time to experience each book in the Titan World series!

Now, I'm happy to introduce you to Tarina Deaton's *Rescued Heart*, where her Combat Hearts series meets the Titan Group in a military romance about a soldier who can't resist his best friend's sister while on assignment.

Thank you to Tarina and all the authors who took time out of their busy writing schedules to participate in this project. I think the result is something truly special for our readers.

Titan Hugs and Happy Reading,
    Cristin Harber

GLOSSARY OF MILITARY TERMS

I use a lot of military terms in *Rescued Heart.* Some of them, you can figure out by context, but some of them require an explanation. Some have multiple meanings and, even in the service, you sometimes have to ask for clarification. To make it easier for you, I've included a definition of the following terms:

C-130: A four-engine turbo-prop military transport aircraft. Special Forces guys like to jump out of the back of them.

Dishdasha: Long, white, ankle-length robe-like garment worn by men in the Middle East.

High-and-tight: Military style haircut. Close cut on the sides, very short on the top.

JSOC: Joint Special Operations Command. Headquartered at Ft. Bragg, NC.

Landstuhl: Landstuhl Regional Medical Center - stop-over for serious casualties from Iraq and Afghanistan before being flown to the United States.

LZ: Landing Zone. Designated spot aircraft (usually helicopters) land.

M-4: Military issue rifle.

NVGs: Night Vision Goggles. Sometimes referred to at nogs.

PT: Physical Training. In the Army it is conducted at some ungodly hour of the morning. May also mean Physical Therapy, depending on how broken your body is.

ROTC: Reserve Officer Training Corps. College based officer training/scholarship program resulting in a military commission.

RPG: Rocket Propelled Grenade. Beloved by insurgent militias the world over.

Ruck: Short for Ruck Sack. Fancy military term for 'backpack'. Usually loaded down with at least fifty pounds of gear. Carried on very long marches, called ruck marches. Long distance hikes conducted by masochists. The Air Force does not do this.

Sand-tabling: A table-top practice of an operation or mission, using a model of the target. Named because it used to be done on tables of sand.

Silkies: Short, thin running shorts. They come in tan, green, and black. Also referred to as "Ranger panties".

SOCOM: Special Operations Command. Parent organization of JSOC and other Special Operations units. Headquartered in Tampa, FL.

Souq: An open air market. Where Carrie runs into Aiden in Sex and the City 2.

Terminal Leave: That magical twilight period when a military service member uses their accumulated leave to practice being a civilian, taken between their last official day of duty and their actual separation/retirement date.

Twenty-two hundred: 10pm. Military clocks run on a twenty-four hour period. An easy way to teach simple math.

UAV: Unmanned Ariel Vehicle. May also be referred to as a drone.

VTC: Video Teleconference. FaceTime for the military.

Wheels up: An abbreviated way of saying take-off time.

Because the wheels are up off the ground. Gotta keep things simple for some of these guys.

XO: Executive Officer. In charge of an Army unit's administrative operations and is usually the second-ranked officer in the unit.

PROLOGUE

Jordan Grant pulled around the corner and parked along the curb a few houses down from the France's house. Damn, he was late. His dad was going to kill him for missing half of his own 'welcome-back-from-college' barbecue. It blew, having to work on his summer vacation, but his ROTC scholarship didn't give him time to work during the school year.

Walking up to the side of the house, he caught a glimpse of Emme's dark curls rounding the corner. Guess he wasn't the only one running late.

"Emme!" She didn't turn around. In fact, it looked like she was trying to avoid him. "Emme, wait up." He broke into a jog as she ran across the yard and headed to the small gazebo in the back.

He stepped into the covered wooden platform. "Emme Lou Who, what you running for?" She kept her back to him. What? No Jordan Jingleballs? "Hey. What's wrong?

She sniffed. "Please go away, Jordan."

What the hell? "Are you crying?" Because he teased her?

Her head shook, sending her mass of curls tumbling across her back, and turned further into the corner.

"""

He sat next to her. "Emme, talk to me."

A sob shook her shoulders and her hands covered her face.

"Do you want me to get your mom?"

She shook her head harder and he caught a whiff of her flowery shampoo. His dick stirred in his jeans. What the hell? Not the right time, not the right person.

"Then talk to me." *And please, god, stop crying.*

"I broke up with my boyfriend," she said in a small voice.

Oh, shit. He leaned a little away from her. "I think you should talk to your mom about this."

"No!" She tilted her face up, tears streaming down her face from her honey-colored eyes. "She'll tell Dad and he'll get angry and do something stupid."

"Okay." He took one of her hands in his. "Then tell me what happened."

"I thought he liked me, but it was just a stupid bet."

"Who? What?"

"David Baker."

His head reared back. "Daniel Baker's brother?"

She nodded.

Damn right she needed to worry about what her dad would do if the little brother was anything like the older brother. "What happened, Emme?"

"He wanted to have sex, but I didn't want to."

Jordan clenched his teeth and tamped down the rage threatening to overtake him. If this story ended up with anything other than that fuckwad saying "all right then", he was going to fucking lose it. "Did he—?"

Her head shook vehemently. "No. He took 'no' for an answer, but he wasn't nice about it." She started crying again. "He called me a tease and said I was nothing but a stuck-up bitch." She ended on a sob.

He wrapped an arm around her shoulders and pulled her into his side. "Emme—"

"That's not even the worst part," she cried. "He said— He said the only reason he asked me out in the first place was because… because the bounty on my virginity is two-hundred dollars." She turned her face into his chest and cried uncontrollably.

That son of a bitch. He was dead.

Jordan wanted to rush into the house, grab Doug, find that asshole, and beat the shit out of him. Instead, he rocked her while he rubbed her back.

"Emme, I want you to listen to me. No guy who says shit like that to you is worth your tears."

"I know. I do, but it still hurts," she said into his chest.

He kissed top of her head then tilted it back. Her eyes were puffy and her nose was red. "You're beautiful and smart and special. One day, you're going to find someone who sees all of that in you and treats you the way you deserve to be treated. It sure as hell isn't going to be an asshole like David Baker."

"You're just saying that."

"Have I ever lied to you?"

She sniffed and took a shuddering breath through parted lips. Her long, spiky lashes framed eyes that had little flecks of green in them. Shit. She *was* beautiful. When had that happened? When had little Emme Lou Who grown up?

He shouldn't notice. She was his best friend's little sister and four years younger. Her gaze dropped to his mouth and he lost his will to fight. He closed the distance between them, giving her time to pull away.

She didn't and he tasted her tears.

It was sweet and chaste, like something out of chick flick. He tried to tell himself it didn't mean anything — he was just comforting her, but a small part of his mind knew he was lying to himself. Kissing Emme was different. Special.

And a mistake that could never happen again.

CHAPTER 1

*E*mmeline France ran the threadbare towel across her forehead, stopping the rivulets of sweat from dripping into her eyes. New drops beaded up along her hairline. The heat of the West African summer was unrelenting and she stared up at the slow-turning aluminum ceiling fans. *Move the air, you useless pieces of metal.*

"Anuli, how many patients are waiting?" The sip of room temperature water did little to cool her down. She grimaced, sick of drinking water. God, she'd pay good money for an iced latte.

"Three, Miss Emme. I think one about to have the baby." Although Anuli's thick, lyrical French and Bambara accent sounded as tired as she looked, she seemed unaffected by the heat.

Emme looked at the clock on the dingy wall. Why did it feel like she'd jammed twenty hours into the last twelve? Go to Africa, they said. It'll be rewarding, they said. It was. But it was also hot, dusty, and incredibly frustrating.

Sometimes it sucked being the only clinic for miles that catered to women and children. "Okay. Take her to room four and get her comfortable. Is she here by herself?"

"Yes."

She sighed and rubbed her eyes. "Close the front door before you take her back. We'll call it a day after these last few."

Pushing to her feet, she braced her hands on her hips and twisted at the waist to crack her lower back. Three more patients and then she could put on some shorts and read a book. Hopefully, she'd stay awake through a full chapter this time.

She walked down the short hall to the waiting room and asked for the next patient. She led the young girl accompanied by an Auntie, an older woman from her village, to one of the exam rooms.

"How are you today?"

"I am good," the girl said.

"My name is Emme. What's yours?"

"Mariam." She sat still on the end of the table, her hands folded in her lap while her Auntie stood next to her.

"It's nice to meet you, Mariam. How can I help you today?"

"I think I am pregnant." Her happiness shone through in her wide smile.

She pulled the stethoscope from around her neck. "How old are you Mariam?"

"Fifteen."

Emme plastered on a smile and died a little inside. *She's too young to be a mother.* "I'm going to listen to your heart and lungs and then we'll do a simple pregnancy test, okay?" The girl nodded and sat up straighter.

She set the stethoscope in her ears and placed the end against the girl's chest. Even after six months in Mali, it bothered her. It didn't matter that the government had made child marriages illegal, tribal culture held more sway in this part of the country.

Shouts erupted from the waiting room. Confused, she pulled the stethoscope from her ears and poked her head out of the curtained-off room. Four armed men rounded the corner, shouting in a mix of French and Tuareg.

What the hell was going on? She stepped out of the room. "You can't be here. *Vous ne pouvez pas être ici.*" They advanced toward her and she held up her hands as if to push them back. "Please, this is a women's clinic. Please leave."

"*Tais-toi! Salope!*" One of the gunmen slammed the butt of his rifle into her temple. Stars exploded behind her eyes. He legs gave out and she crumpled onto the hard, cracked linoleum floor. Pain shot through her shoulder, accompanied by a loud pop, when she hit. The edges of her vision blurred.

Dad is going to have a shit fit. Blackness closed around her.

CHAPTER 2

*J*ordan picked up the ringing phone, never taking his eyes of the situation report he was reading. "Major Grant."

"It's Major Bella. The commander wants to see you."

"Got it. Thanks." He set the receiver back on the cradle. Sitting back in his chair, he rubbed his hands over his high-and-tight and yawned. Christ, he was tired. The dreams had come back in force after the camping trip a month ago and he hadn't been sleeping for shit. Those trips were supposed to be his escape. Get out, shoot the shit with some friends, relax, reminisce about all the stupid shit they'd done early in their careers.

Seeing Bree Marks had thrown him for a loop. Brought back memories he didn't like to remember. If he'd known, he could have prepared himself, but he hadn't expected to see the person who'd help save him and his team. Fuck, he still cringed thinking about what an ass he'd made of himself in front of Bree and his camping buddies.

So much for getting past all his issues — he'd been fooling himself. He needed to get his head in the game and go back out.

Back to the fight. That's where he belonged. The only place the world seemed to make sense anymore.

Sucking back the dregs of coffee, he tossed the cup in the trash before yanking his ID card out of the reader and locking his computer. He took a sharp right out of his office, his movements precise as he walked down the hall to the commander's office.

"Good morning, Betty."

The commander's long-time secretary looked up from her computer screen. "Good morning, Major. Go on in, he's expecting you."

Uh, yup. He nodded, biting back his sarcastic reply. The XO had just called him — stood to reason the commander was expecting him. Rapping twice on the doorframe, he waited.

"Send him in when he gets here." Colonel Bates waved him in and hung up the phone. "Close the door and have a seat, Major Grant."

Jordan sat in one of the well-padded leather chairs opposite the commander's desk.

Colonel Bates folded his hands on top of the desk and leaned forward. "There's no easy way to tell you what I'm about to say, so I won't bullshit you."

His scalp prickled. *Well that's never good.* It wasn't his family — that call would have been direct. Could one of his soldiers have been injured between PT that morning and now?

"You're being pulled off the deployment."

"What?" He fisted his hands on thighs, digging his nails into his palms. The sharp sting helped reign in his anger. "Sir, we're three days away from movement. What the hell? Why?"

The Colonel sighed. "You've been by-name requested."

"For what? By who?"

"By me," a voice said from the door.

Jordan's spun in his chair. He'd been so focused on the Commander, he hadn't heard the door open. The guy who stepped in was tall, built, and carried himself like an operator.

"Who are you?"

"This is Jared Westin," Colonel Bates said. "He's the owner of an organization called The Titan Group."

"Never heard of it," he said. How the hell did a private org have the pull to by-name request him?

"Good." Westin slipped his hands into his pants pockets. "Then we're doing our job."

If he had hair on the back of his neck, it would be standing on end. What the fuck was going on? "And what is your job?"

Westin shrugged. "It depends on the customer. This job is a retrieval mission."

"Retrieval of what?"

"Who. We're retrieving a who."

Jordan growled low in the back of his throat. "Fine," he ground out. "*Who* the hell is so important that you by-name request me and pulled me off a six-month deployment? One we've trained the last three months for."

"It's Emme," a fourth voice said from the doorway.

Why did he look so familiar? He looked a little like… "Doug?" Jordan stood and approached his childhood best friend, disbelief warring with the anger he'd been fighting. Dark circles under his brown eyes accentuated the sallowness of his skin. Man he'd aged in the last ten years, but that didn't explain the stress etched into his face.

He pulled Doug into a strong hug, slapping him on the back. "How're you?"

Doug's hug was half-hearted at best. "Not good." He pressed his lips together in a thin, tight line.

"What's going on? How does this involved Emme?"

"Let's sit down," Colonel Bates said.

Jordan turned. The Colonel stood in front of his desk, indicating the small, round conference table. Jordan pulled out a chair and waited for Doug to sit before taking his seat. The other two joined them.

Doug rested his elbows on the table and ran his fingers roughly through his thick, dark hair before dropping his hands to the table and gripping them together so tight his knuckled turned white.

The deep breath he took shuddered out before he spoke. "Emme's been kidnapped."

"What?" How was that possible? Emme was only…well crap, she had to be in her late twenties, early thirties by now. He leaned forward. "How? By who?"

"She was working in a clinic in eastern Mali. She and three other workers were taken by an armed group," Doug said.

Jordan shook his head. What the hell was she doing in Mali? "I don't—"

"Why don't I explain?" Westin asked.

Doug nodded and looked at Jordan, anguish radiating from his gaze.

"Emme France is a nurse practitioner employed by an NGO, non-government organization, at a clinic in Mali in West Africa." Westin's voice was even, almost detached. "Two weeks ago, she and three women who worked at the clinic were kidnapped by a small group claiming affiliation with al-Murabitun. The al-Murabitun spokesman has denounced the claim, saying it's the work of a small faction not associated with their efforts."

"Why is that important?" He couldn't get the image of a teen with wild hair being kidnapped by terrorists. He had to think about this rationally.

"They don't have the experience to handle the negotiations," Westin said.

Jordan opened his mouth, but caught the subtle shake of Westin's head. He was pulling his punches. Doug didn't have the full story. Why?

Tapping his finger on the table, he studied the man across from him. Leaning back in his chair, Westin had the look of a someone without a care in the world. Jordan recognized the coiled alertness of someone who had the training and skill to dole out death without a qualm. What questions could he ask while keeping Doug in the dark? Westin would damn well give him the full story later.

"They're demanding a ransom?" he asked.

"Yes," Doug said.

He shifted his gaze to Doug. "Why not just pay it?"

Doug blanched. "It's ten million dollars."

"Is that what they started at?

"Yes." He rubbed his eyes. "They're refusing to negotiate for a lower amount."

"Doesn't the NGO usually pay in these situations?

"There's some confusion as to which organization Emme actually works for," Westin said, derision dripping from his voice.

"How do you mean?"

"Technically, she works for a smaller NGO which was subcontracted by a larger, more well-known organization. Her company doesn't have the capital to pay the ransom and the larger NGO is saying she isn't their employee."

What a cluster fuck. No wonder Doug looked like he hadn't slept in, well, two weeks. "Why me? Don't you have the manpower for this type of operation?"

"The family is insisting." Westin spoke as if Doug wasn't sitting next to him.

Jordan looked at his old friend. "Doug?"

"Mom wants someone to go that Emme will know. Dad hired Titan when the NGO said they wouldn't pay the ransom. Dad's been out of the service for so long he may as well be a civilian. The only thing I know about special operations is what I've seen in the movies." He snorted. "Hell, I have a hard time finding my way out of the parking garage at work some days."

He paused, as if to collect his thoughts. "Our moms still talk.

Mom knew you were in the Army and asked your mom where you were. Titan pulled some strings."

"And you're okay with this?" Jordan asked Westin. He couldn't imagine a man who ran a private security company that did retrieval work in West Africa would be copacetic with bringing in an outsider.

His mouth twisted. "My wife was on board."

Jordan looked at Colonel Bates, sitting back letting the conversation unfold.

"The order came from SOCOM directly," the Colonel said. "There are added incentives." He started at Jordan, waiting for him to ask.

He didn't care what they had to offer. Still, he struggled with his conscience. There was no easy answer. Abandon his soldiers or abandon the people who were like a second family to him growing up. This Titan Group would go without him. Would more than likely succeed, if Jared Westin was any indication of the type of people they were. His presence, or lack of, wouldn't determine the outcome of the operation, only provide peace of mind to the Frances.

"Please, Jordan. It's Emme." Doug's voice wavered at the end.

"All right," he said. "I'll do it."

Doug's breath escaped him in a rush and he cradled his head in his hands. "Thank you."

Jordan patted him on the shoulder and leveled his gaze at Westin. "Now what?"

Reaching into the inside breast pocket of his coat, Westin pulled out a business card and slid it across the table. "Twenty-two hundred showtime. Address is on the back. My contact info is on the front. Bring your three-day bag — civilian gear. We'll kit you out."

"Weapons?"

"Unless you have one you prefer, we'll provide those too." He stood and buttoned his coat. "If the operation goes as planned, we'll have you back with your soldiers in under a week."

He glared at Westin's retreating back. Like any operation had ever gone as planned.

CHAPTER 3

Pain exploded in her cheek, layered on top of the other cuts and bruises. Her teeth closed down on the side of her tongue and a metallic taste filled her mouth. She blinked back the tears. *Don't give them the satisfaction.* She'd learned that lesson early on. Her tears only fueled their anger.

Her vision cleared enough to bring the brown adobe walls back into focus. Her captor's sandal-clad feet shuffled on the hard-packed dirt floor.

"Look at the camera! Say the words!" The man's fetid breath washed over her face and she swallowed back the bile that tried to work its way up her throat. His accent was harsh and angry.

She shook her head. She wouldn't say lies that would put other people in jeopardy. Even if it meant the beatings stopped.

Her interrogator hit her open-handed, but with enough force to topple her out of her chair. A whimper escaped. She'd lost count of the number of times she'd landed on her dislocated shoulder. The left side of her face throbbed in time to her heart-beat. Was it too much to ask for a southpaw to give her face a break? Good to know the beatings hadn't affected the sarcastic part of her brain.

Someone behind her yanked up the rickety chair she was tied to and her head lolled forward.

"Hold the chair," the man in front of her said. A hand grabbed the crown of her head and tipped it back. He stared down at her, his obsidian black eyes lit with fury. "You will make the video, whore. One way or the other."

This time he used his fist and her world went black.

∼

Her body jerked. God, she hurt. A single, bright sliver of light unerringly found her one good eye.

Groaning, she tried to turn her head away from the sting of the rough cloth on her battered face. Gentle hands stopped her, accompanied by a soft shushing sound

"Rester, dogomuso."

Be still, little sister? Only Anuli called her little sister.

Emme peered at the speaker. "Anuli." Her voice cracked on the last syllable. It was the first time she'd seen anyone other than her captors. "They took you?" Stupid question. Of course they took her, if she was here. She tried to push up from the dirt floor and another groan escaped.

"No, no, Miss Emme. Lie down. Try not to move."

Her arms gave out, giving her no choice in the matter. "Is there water?"

Anuli shuffled a few steps to the side of the room and returned with a small cup. She slid her hand under Emme's head and raised it enough to allow her to take a sip.

Gagging at the first taste, she choked down the warm, dusty water. Anuli lowered her head and replaced the cup.

"How long have I been unconscious?"

Anuli kneeled next to her. "I'm not sure. They brought you in last night. I was very worried when you didn't wake up."

Christ she hurt. She tried to separate out the worst injuries from the general pain. No doubt her right shoulder was dislocated. She drew in a deep breath and — judging by the pain — a cracked rib or two. Her cheek throbbed — whether from the repeated hits or a fractured cheekbone, she wasn't sure.

Anuli touched the cloth to her face again. She flinched, sending spears of pain down her side.

"Why they beat you so bad, Miss Emme?"

"They want me to make a video. Say the clinic is performing abortions and is a cover for the American government."

"These are bad men, Miss Emme." She shuffled out of sight. When she returned, she carried the cup and a small piece of bread. She dipped the bread into the water to soften it and held it to Emme's mouth. "Eat."

"Help me sit up, please."

"You should rest."

"I can't eat laying down."

Anuli tsk'd, but helped her sit and prop herself against the rough mud brick wall. She bit back a groan, concentrating on taking shallow breaths.

She scanned the small room — no more than eight feet square. A metal bucket sat on a rickety looking table. Another bucket sat in the far corner. Thankfully, nature wasn't calling at the moment. A narrow window near the ceiling revealed only blue sky. She'd take a better look when she didn't feel like passing out just from sitting against the wall.

Tearing off a piece of the crusty flat bread, she dipped it into the cup and mashed the soggy bread to the roof of her mouth. Her tongue had that thick, raw feel to it from when she'd bitten the side. "I'm sorry you got dragged into this."

"Not your fault. They took Amara and Sarah too."

She stopped chewing and closed her eyes. *Shit.* "Did they take any others?"

"I don't think so. They kept me with the other two until last night. They brought me in here and told me to fix you." Her eyes became sad. "You are the only one they've beaten."

"I'm the only white woman." She accepted another piece of bread Anuli offered her.

"Maybe they won't hit you if you make the video."

Not likely. "They'll find something to beat me for even if I make the video."

"You have to do something, Miss Emme. They'll kill you if they beat you again."

"They won't. They want the ransom." She hoped her voice sounded more sure than she felt. Her eyes stung as she blinked back the tears.

It was too much money. The NGO wasn't going to pay it and her family sure as hell couldn't afford ten million dollars. Even as a retired one-star, her dad didn't have that kind of collateral.

Tears spilled over. She brushed them away. *That's not going to help.* "How long have we been here?"

Anuli looked at the sliver of daylight filtering in through the small window. "Jum'ah was three or four days ago."

"Was that the only one since we've been taken?"

"The second."

Two Fridays. They'd been taken on a Wednesday, so they'd been in captivity for two weeks. *Think, Emme.* "Did you hear the call to prayer?"

Anuli shook her head. "No. We could hear the men praying in the other room." She pointed at the high window.

If Anuli didn't hear the call to prayer, they weren't near a village. Even the smallest village played the call to prayer. "Do you know where they took us?"

Another head shake. "They put bags over our heads. We drove for a long time. The sun was setting when we arrived here."

She needed a plan. Something to keep her mind on. Wait or try to escape? What to do?

"W2D2?" Doug's voice whispered in her mind. *What Would Dad*

Do? She smiled and winced when her lip split. Their inside joke as kids. They'd ask each other "W2D2" whenever they found themselves in tight spot or needed to figure something out. What would her special-operations, combat-veteran father do?

Anything it takes.

He'd move heaven and earth to get her. Pull in every marker and call every contact he had. Hell, she wouldn't put it past him to go through the back of *Soldier of Fortune* magazine and call every two-bit, mercenary wanna-be if it meant getting her out alive.

All she had to do was stay alive.

CHAPTER 4

$\mathcal{A}$ guard stepped out of the shack outside the small private airstrip on the south side of Fayetteville, North Carolina. Dressed in black tactical gear with an M-4 slung tight across his chest, he was no rent-a-cop.

Jordan pulled to a stop and rolled down his window. "Jordan Grant."

"ID, please."

He pulled out his wallet and handed over his ID. The guard looked at it, peered at him, then glanced in the back of the pickup's cab.

"Follow the perimeter road around to the right. Park in front of the third hangar and leave the keys on the dash. Your flight is waiting for you."

Where the hell am I? He took his ID card "Roger. Thanks." He waited for the chain-link gate to slide clear before pulling forward. Parking in front of the hangar, he drummed his thumb on the steering wheel, and stared at the civilian helicopter through the rearview mirror. What kind of pull did these guys have? Private, guarded airfield outside Fayetteville he didn't even know existed. Multi-million dollar helicopter ready to go.

General France had nothing but good things to say about Jared Westin and Titan Group. The General had known Westin when he was fresh out of Ranger training and had kept tabs on him since. He was the only person the General had called when he decided to stop relying on the officials to handle the situation. Every other contact Jordan had called, who knew who Titan were, told him the same thing. They were legit.

He turned off the ignition and threw the keys on the dash. Getting out, he grabbed his ruck sack and weapons case from the back of his truck and made his way to the helicopter twenty yards in front of the hangar.

The pilot exited as he approached. "Jordan Grant?"

"Yes."

"Rocco Savage." He shook Jordan's hand. "That all the gear you have?"

"Yeah." He adjusted his ruck on shoulder. "What's going to happen to my truck?"

Rocco opened the rear sliding door of the helicopter. "It'll be safe here for now. Once we know when and where you'll return, we'll arrange for it to be there for you."

Chauffeur service for his truck. Another thing to add to the list of strings these guys could pull. He threw his bag and weapons case on the floor of crew area, climbed into the co-pilot seat, and buckled his harness. Rocco handed him a set of earphones and started the engines.

"You fly?" Rocco asked.

He shook his head and watched Rocco go through the start up. "Only as a passenger. And I'm usually in the back, not in the front."

"Totally different view up front. The flight to DC is about two hours. You can catch some zzz's if you need to."

The rotors whined to life and the helo shimmied as the engines revved. The lift off was smooth and slow as Rocco asked for clearance from air traffic control. The sleek machine rose, its nose slightly down as they moved forward before gaining altitude. Jordan watched the lights of the airfield fall away as they sped away.

"Do you know what the plan is?" He looked at Rocco.

Rocco glanced over at him. "We're waiting on some final intel. Once we get to DC, we'll have about an hour on the ground before we take off. Jared's holding off on the full brief until you're on the ground."

"How long have you been with Titan?"

"A few years. Jared recruited me out of Special Forces."

"You like it?"

Rocco grinned. "Love it, man."

"Why?"

"You're a Ranger, right?" Rocco glanced at him and then watch his flight instruments.

"Yeah."

"You ever go out on a mission and realize there was no point to it? Sure, you shwacked some bad guys, but it didn't actually accomplish anything."

"Yeah, a few times." Every fucking mission in Iraq and Afghanistan had left him more and more disillusioned. His soldiers were what was important. The guy or gal to his left and right. If not for them, he'd have been out of the Army a long time ago.

"Never happens. Every mission we take has a clear objective. We don't always solve the larger problem, but we sure as hell put a huge mother fucking dent in it."

Jordan looked out into the inky-black night. What would that be like?

~

*T*he skids touched down gently, with the slightest jar. He twisted the release on his harness and waited for Rocco to shut the engine down. Grabbing his gear from the back, he followed Rocco into the hangar. A gray C-130 aircraft filled the large space, the crew stairs down and waiting for passengers.

Rocco led him to the second briefing room where Westin, two guys, and a leather clad, bombshell of a woman stood around a conference table. A bank of computer monitors hung on the wall at their backs, various maps with mission planning overlays displayed on two of them. He set he gear down as Westin caught his eye.

"Jordan Grant, this is Colby Winters and Cash Garrison." He exchanged head nods as Westin indicated each man. "They'll be on the team with us. You met our pilot, Rocco. This is our weapons specialist, Sugar and Parker's on VTC somewhere."

"I'm here." A disembodied voice sounded from the computers. Seconds later a face appeared on the middle of the five screens. "We ready?"

"Go," Westin said.

"Emmeline France. Goes by Em-*ee*. Thirty-one years old. Undergrad from UNC-Chapel Hill, M.S. as a family nurse practitioner. Briefly married at twenty-three but divorced two years later. She worked three years at various hospitals in the Carolinas and Virginia before she began working for the NGO Medical Relief United in 2014. Six months ago MRU was contracted by a larger, global NGO to run the women's clinic in Gao, Mali."

Various pictures flashed on the far right screen during Parker's narrative. Jeez, little Emme had grown up. She had the same eyes as her brother, but hers were more golden than brown and shone bright in her sweetheart face.

Parker continued. "This was the proof of life al-Murabitun sent a few days after they raided the clinic." The next picture showed a bruise high on her temple with blood matted in her hair. Dark circles hung heavy under her eyes and the twinkle, so evident in all her other pictures, was missing.

His gut clenched. His breathing increased and he had the overwhelming urge to beat the ever-living crap out of something. Or someone.

"Jesus," Sugar said. "When was that picture taken?"

"Two weeks ago," Parker said.

"Nothing since?"

"No."

"Shit," she whispered. "How do we know she's still alive?"

Westin slipped an arm around her waist and pulled her close. "The group is still trying to negotiate as if she is. They've made threats of sending body parts, which is why the family contacted us." He pressed his mouth against her temple.

The moment was intimate and he felt intrusive and uncomfortable watching. No one else seemed to find it out of the norm, however.

"One way or the other, Baby Cakes, she's coming home." Westin released her and said, "Parker, let us know if there're any updates," before turning back to the group. He looked at Jordan. "You good?"

No. He was not good. All he could picture was the gangly little girl who used to tag along after him and Doug. Planting his feet, he crossed his arms. "What haven't you told the Frances?" He glared at Westin.

Westin matched his stance. Jordan refused to break first. He wasn't going to kowtow to anyone. He didn't give two shits what kind of reputation they had.

Sugar decided the outcome when she smacked Westin on the chest with the back of her hand. "Quit it and tell the man what he needs to know."

Westin leveled a flat 'we'll talk about this later' look at her.

Sugar winked in response and Jordan looked at his boots to hide his smile.

"Emme France may have been targeted."

His head snapped up. "What?"

"She maintains a blog," Westin said.

"Okay."

"She's passionate about women's issues."

He raised his eyes to the high ceiling of the hangar. "For fuck's sake, spit it out."

Someone started choking on a cough. "Sorry," Winters wheezed. "Dot went down the wrong pipe."

"Look man, I get it. You're top dog. When it comes time, I'll take orders like a good soldier," Jordan said. "But right now is not that time. Spell it out."

Westin dropped his arms and braced his hands on the table. "She may have caught the attention of this group because of the content of her blog and video blog."

"It's called a vlog, boss," Rocco said. Westin glared at him and Rocco threw his hands up. "Sorry."

"Why do you think that?" Jordan asked.

"Parker dug into her blog. There were a lot of deleted comments — threats, warnings to stop, general 'death to America' comments — that sort of thing."

One of the computers chimed and Cash reached over and hit a key. Parker's face appeared on the screen. "We got satellite and new proof of life. Which one you want first?"

"Proof of life." Sugar and Jordan spoke at the same time.

"Coming up now."

The camera was shaky, obviously hand-held. A woman sat tied to a chair. Lank, dirty hair obscuring her face. Two guards, visible from the chest down, stood behind the chair, AK-47s gripped tight in their hands. A hand reached out and pushed the woman's head back.

The collective gasps could have sucked the air out of the hangar. One of her eyes was swollen shut. Livid bruising covered the left side of her face and blood caked around her nostrils.

A heavily accented voice sounded from the video. "This is what happens when you don't pay. No more talking. You have forty-eight hours to send the ransom or she dies."

The screen when black.

"Fuck!" Rage boiled up through him. He had to move. Slamming out of the room, he stood on the landing of the stairs. He needed something to punch. Gripping the cold, metal railing he shook it. When they got there, he was going to rip every one of them apart with his bare hands. Reach into their chests and tear out their hearts. The image of her tied to that chair was seared onto the back of his retinas. God, when her mom and dad saw that video… Shit.

He ripped the door open and stormed back into the office. "Please tell me her family hasn't seen that."

"No," Parker said. "It's sitting in the inbox of the negotiator's email."

"Kill it," he demanded. "Her parents can't see it. Ever."

"Make it look like it was delivered," Westin said. "Then erase it."

"Copy. I'll analyze it. See if I can pull anything useful," Paker said.

"What's the intel?" Westin asked.

Parker looked at the camera. "We have eyes on the compound."

"In the building?" Jordan asked.

"Unfortunately, no." Parker said. "But almost as good."

One of the screens switched to an overhead view of a walled compound. It reminded him of the old PAC-MAN game grid — straight lines indicating walls, openings that were likely doorways. Distinct red dots moved around the compound. Occasionally a line would appear from the dots. An arm?

He'd never seen a sensor like this. He moved around the table, closer to the screen. "Is this satellite or UAV?"

"UAV," Westin said.

"Where did you get this?"

He looked at Jordan. "It's R and D."

Research and development? What the hell? Why wasn't this technology fielded to troops on the ground? He shook his head. Not an argument he had time for right now.

He looked at the screen again. "What are we looking at?"

Parker spoke from the screen. "The red forms are heat signatures. Looks like they've got some goats around the compound. There's four guards inside the walls." A yellow cursor appeared on the screen and hovered over the forms on the screen. "There're three separate rooms — here, here, and here." The cursor followed his words. "Two heat signatures in this room and this room, with one outside the door. Probably guards. Looks to be about a dozen in this room with another guard outside. There's three signatures in this room. My guess is guards given there aren't any outside the room."

"What's with the group of signatures?" Cash asked.

"Hang on." Parker disappeared from the screen briefly. "I have a search running. You'll have the video feed part of the time you're in transit and again shortly after you land." He looked over to the side. "Boss, you're not going to like this."

"What?" Westin asked.

"Reports are coming in that a group of girls was taken three days ago from a school close to the clinic Emme was grabbed from."

Sugar and Winters started talking at once, saying the same thing — they had to rescue the girls, they couldn't leave them there.

Panic built low in Jordan's chest. No diversions. He understood their outrage, but Emme was the mission. The priority.

"Stop," Westin ordered. "Parker, who's in the area?"

"Hang on," he slid off screen again.

"What about Delta?" Rocco asked.

"They're not available."

Parker slid back into view. "Leonidas has a team in Niger."

"Contact them. See if they can support."

"On it."

"Make sure everything is available on the plane." Westin looked at his watch. "Wheels up in thirty-minutes. We need to get Jordan kitted-out and load up. Make sure we have a schematic of the compound and overview of surround areas — electro-optical and infrared."

"Did you bring personal weapons?" Sugar asked Jordan.

He looked down at her. "Yes."

"Let me see 'em."

He cocked an eyebrow.

"I wouldn't argue if I were you," Cash said. "You'll lose."

He sighed, but picked up his weapons case off the floor, laid it on the table, and thumbed the combination. After snapping the lid open, he stepped to the side.

Sugar pushed in the hinge pins of his M-4 and cracked the stock open. After a quick field check and functions check, she laid it back down and inspected his Glocks. Shaking his head, he watched her handle his weapons like a pro. He should know by now not to underestimate a woman. Bree and Denise had proved that.

She stopped, gun gripped in one hand, slide held back with the other. "What?"

He shook his head again. "Nothing. Just thinking I shouldn't judge a book by its cover."

"How's that?" She released the slide and set the gun down.

"Well." He crossed his arms and rocked back on his heels. "You look like you should be on the cover of a retro pinup girl calendar, not on the cover of *Guns and Ammo*."

"Who says I'm not on both?" She winked.

"Quit flirting, Sugar," Westin said, without looking away from the monitor he was working at.

"Spoil sport," she quipped. "Come on, hot stuff. Let's get you some ammo and gear." He followed her down the stairs, to a chain link gate that divided the far side of the hangar into a storage area. Metal lockers lined the wall and she opened several, revealing row upon row of guns and various other weapons. Pulling out several drawers of an industrial sized tool box, she pulled out ammo and magazines.

"Take what you need. Minimum full combat load. The way these boys go in, I'd take more if I were you. What size vest do you wear?"

"Huh?" He felt like Arnold Schwarzenegger in *Commando* when he broke into the gun store. All that was missing was the RPG launcher. Nope, there it was.

Sugar chuckled and repeated her question.

"Large." In the end he walked out with body armor, helmet, tactical radio, NVGs, thigh and vest holder for his hand guns, two tactical knives, and a partridge in a pear tree. All new. All top of the line. He wasn't an ammo sexual by any means, but even he had a semi.

"Rocco's done with pre-flight. Let's load up." Westin passed him and stopped at Sugar. Jordan kept walking, not wanting to intrude on their goodbye.

He grabbed his gear and climbed the stairs of the aircraft. Jesus. This was not the standard jump seat set up. The front half of the plane was tricked out like the interior of private jets he'd only seen in the movies. Plush, dark brown leather captain's chairs arranged around small tables. It looked like the back of the passenger area was set up for bunks.

Cash approached from the back and reached for his weapons case. "We'll put this in the cargo area. Take anything out of your ruck you want up here and I'll take that as well."

Setting his ruck on one of the chairs, he pulled out his laptop and earphones before handing his bag off. Cash exited through a door at the back of the passenger area and Jordan caught a glimpse of the cargo compartment — and the AH-6 helicopter in the back. "Jesus. Is that a Little Bird?"

Cash looked toward the back of the plane and grinned. "We aren't walking from Timbuktu."

CHAPTER 5

*J*ordan gave up on sleep. He was too keyed up, his mind going a mile a minute. It wasn't unusual before a big op. The night before a normal mission, he slept like a baby, but anything major and he couldn't shut off the part of his brain that thought of every possible scenario and anything that could go wrong.

They'd spent the first two hours sand-tabling the mission, going over comms and signals. Westin had received word that Leonidas, another private security company, would be able to assist them with the take-down of the compound and retrieval of the school girls, allowing Titan to focus on recovering Emme.

Opening his laptop, he connected to the plane's wifi and searched for Emme's blog. Her most recent post had been from three weeks ago, just before her kidnapping. She wrote about the importance of education for young girls in the country and how the terrorist groups were trying to close schools and intimidate villages. Browsing through older posts, he clicked on a link that took him to her YouTube page.

"Hey, everyone. It was a tough day today and I don't really have the

35

energy to write about it, so I figured I'd share in person. Or as in person as a video can be."

Her smile was tight and her eyes were full of weariness.

"A girl came in today. And I do mean girl. She was only fourteen or fifteen years old. She had a miscarriage at three months. She was worried her husband would beat her for losing the baby." She rested her chin on her hand and looked off in the distance for several seconds. She sighed and looked back at the camera. *"I've been here for four months and I still can't fathom it. I think about girls her age back in the States and their biggest concern is how many Twitter followers they have. Hell, when I was fifteen my biggest concern was a boy calling me a stuck-up tease."* She looked down at the table and a wistful smile played at her mouth. *"I had someone who made me realize my worth was my own. I controlled it, not someone else and definitely not someone else's opinion of me. These girls don't have that. I want to give it to them, but I don't know how."*

He paused the video. She was talking about him. And their one and only kiss.

Staring at the screen, he recognized the girl he'd kissed all those years ago. Even though she looked like she carried the weight of the world on her shoulders, Emme *now* was more beautiful. Her long lashes swept her cheeks and freckles dotted her nose. Her dark, curly hair was piled high on her head and he wondered if it still felt as soft as it had back then.

He'd avoided her the rest of that summer and the next two summers after that. Their kiss had made him realized she'd grown up at some point. He couldn't look at her and see the little girl who'd chased after him and Doug. The one he'd teased and whose braids he'd pulled. Out of respect for her father and brother, he'd stayed away. But he'd always wondered what would have happened if he'd been given the chance to kiss her again.

Westin sat in the chair across from him. Jordan took off his earphones and closed his laptop.

"You going to take it?"

Jordan's brow crinkled. "Take what?"

"The promotion."

"What promotion?

Westin started at him, not saying anything.

He rolled his eyes. "Dude, seriously. You really need to be a little more forth coming with the words. I have no idea what you're talking about."

"Your commander told you there were extra incentives for taking the job," Westin said.

"I didn't ask what they were. I didn't care."

Westin continued to stare at him as he ran his fingers over his lips and didn't say anything for several seconds. "When we recover her, we'll leave immediately for Abu Dhabi. We have a doctor on standby to take a look at her. General and Mrs. France have agreed to stay in the States and let the furor of her rescue die down before we transport her back. Two weeks minimum, but it could be longer." He folded his hands across his stomach. "I told them I would ask you, but if you'd prefer to catch up with your unit, I can arrange for someone else—"

"I'll stay with her." Shit, what was he doing? Twelve hours ago, all he wanted to do was go forward with this unit, to get back to what he knew. Now he'd volunteered for babysitting duty. What the fuck?

He got a knowing look. "That will also give her time to recover before she has to travel so far and us time to arrange new passports." Westin stood. "We'll only be in Rabat long enough to refuel. It's three hours to Mali. We'll have about six hours on the ground before we go. Part of that will be hooking up with Leonidas and going over any possible changes to the plan. We'll get your girl."

"She's not my girl."

Westin smirked like he knew something Jordan didn't. "Maybe not yet."

Maybe not ever. Love and commitment didn't seem to be in

the cards for him. Not because he didn't believe in it — Jase and Bree had shown him it existed — he just wasn't sure he could let someone care for him that deeply. He'd gone to too many funerals, watched too many widows and children drowning in grief to ever put someone in that position. It was bad enough his parents had to live with that possibility every time he deployed.

He shook his head, closed his laptop, and reclined his seat. It wasn't something he needed to worry about anyway. He hadn't seen Emme in more than fifteen years. She wouldn't even recognize him.

~

Jordan stared at the horizon. He'd never seen anything like it. The setting sun painted the endless African sky in reds, oranges, and golds.

Westin stepped next to him. "Fuck, I hate this continent."

Jordan raised his eyebrows.

"Long story. Comms are up. The Leonidas team is a few minutes out."

He nodded. "Who are they again?"

Westin crooked his head and led the way back into the squat, sand colored building. "Another private security firm. The owner is Aiden Graham. Retired SEAL. One of the few groups I trust."

"Aww, Westin. I didn't know you cared."

A large, bald man strode through the doorway, ducking down to avoid hitting his head. A dark beard, shot through with gray, covered the lower part of his face.

"I don't, you asshole. Doesn't mean I don't trust you." The two men shook hands.

Jordan held out his hand. "I'd say nice to meet you, but circumstances being what they are..."

Graham took his hand and raised his dark eyebrows. "Understand completely. You new to Titan? I don't remember Westin mentioning you before."

Jordan smirked. "Uh, no. I was appropriated from JSOC."

Graham cocked an eyebrow at Westin. "You're stealing from the Army now?"

He shrugged his shoulders. "He's on loan at the request of the family."

Graham looked doubtful, but turned to the three men and one woman who followed him in. "Let me introduce you to the rest of the team. Turner Breslin, our pilot. Jeremy Owens, weapons and explosives, Harrison Byer, sharp shooter extraordinaire. And Paige Davis, Mistress of Mayhem in general. Don't let her looks fool you, she'd just as soon cut you as look at you." The woman in question rolled her eyes and flipped Graham the bird.

The group dropped their gear in the corner and gathered around the small table covered in printouts of maps and overhead imagery of the compound and surrounding area.

Westin pulled the largest overview from the pile and placed it on top. "Graham, you and your team will insert southwest of the compound, Titan will insert to the northeast." He pointed out the designated points on the map. "We'll breach the main gate and the southwest wall simultaneously. Intel indicates there are less than a dozen guards in the compound, but be prepared for more."

"What kind of weapons do they have?" Owens asked.

"Unknown," Westin said. "But expect the usual — AKs, hand guns, maybe a few RPGs."

The two teams went over the plan several times, until everyone had it set in their heads. Leonidas would have the more difficult job of loading the group of hostages onto their helicopter and transporting them to the United Nations camp in Timbuktu. Even though the girls were reported to be from the same area as Emme's clinic, they felt that was the better option to get them to safety.

Four hours later, Jordan shrugged into his vest and slug his rifle across his chest.

"Any questions?" Westin asked. Everyone remained silent. "Weapons hot. Let's load up."

They stalked out to the helicopters — the AH-6 Titan had brought and the UH-60 Leonidas had arrived on. Jordan perched on the edge of the crew opening, clipped his last-resort belt onto the tether, and braced his feet on the skids. The ground fell away as they lifted on. As soon as they cleared the outskirts of the airfield, he flipped his NVGs down and scanned his field of view.

"Comms check. Titan-one, check," Westin called over the radio.

"Titan-two, check."

"Titan-three, check."

"Titan-four? Check." He looked at Colby next to him and got thumbs up and grin in return.

"Three minutes to LZ." Rocco's calm voice came over his headset.

He shifted his neck side-to-side and took a few deep breaths. Focus. Just a normal mission. Nothing he hadn't done a hundred times before. Didn't matter who the hostage was.

"Thirty seconds."

Rocco descended to the landing zone fast and the ground approached quickly until they were a mere foot above the earth.

He unclipped his D-ring and jumped into the cloud of dust kicked up by the rotor blades. Six steps away, he took a knee, scanning his quadrant for activity. The helo lifted away. They jogged to their rally point, a hundred yards from the compound, and took prone positions.

"Titan set," Westin said.

"Leonidas one minute out."

"Chop chop, Graham. You're getting slow in your old age."

"Bite me, Westin. We had to divert around a heard of goats."

"Baaaa," Cash said.

"That's a sheep you ass."

"Glad you know your farm animals."

Jordan chuckled at easy banter between the two teams.

"Head in the game," Westin admonished, although Jordan could hear the laughter in his voice as well.

"Leonidas set."

"Clear on the north and east," Colby said.

"Clear on the south and west."

"Green light."

They popped up on Westin's call and fell into a small wedge formation with Winters on point and Cash pulling up the rear. Jordan kept his weapon at the ready as they closed the distance to the corrugated metal gate that was their breach point. He took position behind Winters to the left of the door, Westin and Cash on the other side.

Cash set the explosives on the door and returned to his position. Each two-man team hugged the wall as they moved a few feet out of the blast zone.

"Titan is a go," Westin said. "Leonidas, call the countdown when ready."

"Roger. In five...four...three..."

CHAPTER 6

Emme sat cross-legged against the rough adobe wall. A three-day reprieve and she could see out of her eye. She pushed her shoulders back against the wall and hissed in a breath. Shit, that hurt. She foresaw surgery in her future. Anuli had tried to reset her shoulder, but she couldn't get the leverage she needed.

She stared down at the small bowl of rice in her lap, trying to fight against the queasiness enough to eat. Using her fingers she picked up two grains of rice. *One-ninety-three. One-ninety-four. Guess that's one way to avoid heartburn.* What else was she going to do to pass the time?

A wave of heat washed through her along with nausea. She glanced at Anuli. "I think you should try to escape without me." She rested her head against the wall and breathed against the urge to vomit.

Anuli shook her head, like she had the first time Emme'd brought up the idea. They'd discussed escaping together, but neither wanted to leave the other two women.

"No, Emme. They will hurt you worse if I leave."

She shook her head. "They would hurt you if I left. They won't do anything to me if you escape."

The lock scraped as rusted iron slid against rusted iron. They both looked up. No one came after dinner.

The leader, who she'd started referring to as Bob the Breather, stormed into the room yelling. "Get up! Get up!" His minions grabbed her, spilling her bowl of rice. Pain shot through her as they yanked her up. She tried to get her feet under her to lessen the pull on her shoulder.

What the hell is going on? Fear turned her stomach and she swallowed back the rice that tried to find its way up her throat. *Fuck. Fuck. Fuck. Something's wrong.*

Anuli stood and tried to stop them. Minion One hit her in the gut with his gun and pushed her down.

They dragged Emme down the hall and into the room they beat her in. Thrown into the chair, she almost toppled over. One of them tied her hands behind her back, wrenching her shoulder even more.

"What's going on?" Why were they doing this? Even when they beat her, it was methodical. She knew what to expect and could prepare for it. This was…frantic.

Minion Two picked up the video camera and pointed it at her. Bob the Breather grabbed a rough looking machete from beside the door and hefted it as he approached her.

She struggled against the ropes that bound her wrists, her breathing rapid and out of control. "No."

"Your government has had their chance to get you back alive. Now they will take us serious. Allahu Akbar."

"Allahu Akbar," his minions echoed.

No! A sob tore through her. "Please. They need more time." It wasn't supposed to end like this. Why hadn't they negotiated for her release? Where was the cavalry? The inappropriate part of her brain decided to kick in. *This is going to hurt like a bitch. That knife is dull as fuck.*

The blade rose over her head. Another sob escaped and she squeezed her eyes closed.

Pleasegod, pleasegod, pleasegod.

God answered her prayer in a violent explosion, sending dust and small chunks of mud plaster raining down on them.

Emmecracked her good eye open and coughed from the dust filling the room. Holy crap, that couldn't have been timed better if it had been scripted for an action movie. *Thank you, god.*

Her captors yelled to each other and the leader gestured Minion One out of the room. He yanked the door open and stuck his head out before going into the hall, closing it behind him. Bob and the other minion took up positions facing the door.

The *pop pop pop* of gunfire could be heard from the hall. Time seemed to slow in anticipation of who would come through the door.

Please let it be the good guys.

The door flew open and she hunched forward as far as possible.

Three shots, followed by two dull thuds. Silence echoed where once there was chaos. She held her breath, afraid to look.

~

Jordan holstered his Glock and knelt in front of Emme while Westin and Cash checked to make sure the final two captors were out of commission.

Her head drooped, her dirty, lank hair hanging like a curtain. His chest constricted. *Fuck, let her be alive.*

Colby flicked open a knife and cut her bindings.

Jordan's fingers trembled as he tilted her chin up. She blinked and relief flooded through him. Even dirty and covered in grime, he recognized her. "Emme Lou Who? Is that you?"

Her weak slap took him by surprise, but it still stung. "That's my girl."

"Jordan?"

"Hey, Emme Lou."

"Quit calling me that, Jingle Balls."

He grinned. "You ready to go home?"

Tears pooled and spilled over, streaking through the dust and grime on her face. "Yes." A sob wracked her body.

He brushed away a tear, wishing he had the time to gather her close and brush them all away. "Can you walk?" He stood and helped her up.

"I think so. We need to get Anuli." She rose and swayed, but kept her feet.

"Who's Anuli?" Jordan took her left elbow, careful of her right arm hanging limp by her side.

"The nurse who was taken with me. There's two other girls, too."

She stumbled and he swept her into his arms. He followed Colby and Jared, depending on them to keep the path clear. They stopped outside the room they'd found the first two girls in, where they'd told the other woman to go to.

One of the women rushed to them. "Miss Emme! You hurt again?"

"I'm okay Anuli. Just light-headed." Her forehead tucked under his chin was burning up. He held her trembling body closer. *Please let this be adrenaline crash and not something more serious.*

"Follow the men." He pointed with his chin. Anuli brushed her hand against Emme's cheek before following the other two girls.

Westin called over the radio to Rocco for pickup. The small helo set down feet from the destroyed entrance. Colby and Cash ushered the girls toward the helicopter, but they stopped and refused to go further.

"What's the problem?" Westin asked, impatience evident in his voice.

"They are afraid of the helicopter," Anuli said. "They think you will take them far away."

"We just rescued them. Why would we—? Never mind. Tell them we're taking you back to Gao. They can either go with us or find their own way."

Jordan carried Emme to the helicopter and laid her down on the litter they'd prepared before take-off. He buckled the straps, ensuring they were snug but not tight.

"You good?" He had to raise his voice over the engine noise. She nodded and closed her eyes as a shiver shook her body. Anuli clambered in behind him and sat cross-legged next to Emme. He grabbed the tether closest to her and snapped it onto his D-ring. Keying up his mic he asked, "What about the other two women?"

Cash answered. "They decided to walk back to their village." He clipped in next to Jordan and tilted his head toward Anuli. "This one said she'd go with Emme."

Westin climbed in to the co-pilot seat for the return trip. "Leonidas, come in."

"Leonidas here."

"Status check."

"Good to go. All the girls are loaded up. We're headed for the U.N. camp in Timbuktu."

"Roger. Thanks for your help, Graham."

"Anytime, Westin."

The flight back to the airfield seemed half as long as the flight out. Euphoria, brought on by adrenaline and the success of the mission, flooded his veins.

He glanced over his shoulder at Emme for the tenth time. Anuli held her hand. She was in better condition than he'd expected based on the video they'd seen, but the fever wasn't good.

They set down close to the tail of the airplane, the engine shutting down almost immediately. He unhooked from the tether, then unbuckled Emme.

"Mister." Anuli touched his arm. "Thank you." She threw her

arms around his neck and hugged him. He didn't have time to do more than raise his hands before she let him go and bent over Emme. "Take care, *dogomuso*. I will always remember you."

He stopped her as she climbed out of the helicopter. "Will you be all right?"

"Yes. I have family here. They will help me." She looked back at Emme. "Take care of her. She is very special." Patting him on his arm, she lowered herself to the ground and walked away.

He picked Emme up and handed her down to a waiting Colby. "She's passed out and shaking."

"We've got medical supplies on board." Colby led the way up the rear ramp into the crew area and laid her down on the medevac litter set up on the back wall.

Jordan grabbed the large EMT bag and began pulling out the supplies to run an I.V., setting them up on her legs so Colby had easy access to them. They worked in concert and had Emme hooked up to saline and a broad spectrum antibiotic within minutes.

"Stay with her." Colby shoved the bag under the bed. "I'm going to help them finish loading the Little Bird."

"No, I'll help load. We'll get out of here faster."

They loaded the plane and were wheels up in less than an hour. He dropped into the chair closest to Emme and watched her steady breathing under the blanket tucked around her body, only her head and arm with the I.V. visible.

Exhaustion pressed down on him. He rested his elbows on his knees and dropped his head into his hands. Fuck. He needed to call her parents.

A hand squeezed his shoulder and he lifted his head. Westin stood over him. "These seats recline almost horizontal. There's a button on the side."

Jordan shook his head. "I need to call General France."

"I sent a message to Parker. He's going to let them know. It's an eight-hour flight to Abu Dhabi. Get some sleep."

He nodded once and looked for the button as Westin strode toward the front of the plane. Reclining the seat, he turned his head to keep Emme in sight as his blinks became longer and longer.

CHAPTER 7

*E*mme's bladder felt like it might explode. She opened her eyes and blinked several times. The opulence of the room was evident, even in the defused light created by the closed blinds and sheer curtains. The cream comforter under her hand was soft and luxurious. Where the hell was she? She closed her eyes. The last thing she remembered was the machete arching above her head and the explosion.

Jordan. She blinked her eyes several times. Was that a dream? How did she get here, wherever 'here' was?

Her immediate needs were more pressing. She pushed herself up with one arm, the other immobile against her side. Staring down at the cotton nightgown, she pulled the neck away and peeked at her shoulder. It ached, but no longer hurt like it was out of socket. Someone had wrapped it and taken the extra precaution of securing her arm to her body.

She threw back the covers and swung her feet to the floor, trying to determine which of the three doors was the bathroom. The farthest one likely led out of the room. She swayed for a moment, before finding her balance. Door one led to a large walk-in closet, filled with men's and women's clothes. Whose house was she in? That closet was bigger than the bedroom of her first apartment. Shaking her head, she closed the door and tried door number two.

She was dead and this was heaven. That was the only explanation. The opulence of the bedroom carried over to the spa-like bathroom. A large, deep soaking tub and steam shower took up the back half of the bathroom. Shiny marble topped the his and hers vanities. Maybe there was an extra toothbrush. Of course there would be. This was heaven. Although she probably wouldn't have fuzzy teeth in heaven or have to pee.

She sat on the toilet and looked to her right at the bidet. Europe? Rubbing at her ears, she tried to make them pop. She didn't feel any pain, so her eardrum was probably fine. She'd ask whoever had wrapped her shoulder to look at them, just to be sure.

Someone knocked on the door and she jumped. "Miss France?" a woman asked.

Wide-eyed, she stared at the door. Was she supposed to have stayed in bed? "Yes?"

"Are you all right? Do you need assistance?"

She could hear a slight British accent in the woman's voice. "No. I'm just using the facilities." She cringed at having to tell a stranger she was peeing.

"All right. I'll be out here if you need anything."

"Uh. Okay. Thank you." What was she supposed to need? Other than answers. She flushed, shuffled to the vanity, and washed her hands. Searching through the drawers, she found an unopened travel toothbrush and toothpaste. *I am in heaven.* She stared down at the vanity while scrubbing the fuzz off her teeth, an awkward thing to do left-handed. Using one of the glasses on the vanity, she rinsed then drank two full glasses.

A blissful sigh escaped. Water had never tasted so good.

She'd kept her eyes averted the entire time, but the urge became overwhelming. Pressing her lips together, she looked at her face in the mirror. No longer swollen shut, the area under her eye was still discolored. The fading yellow and brown bruises on her cheekbone looked like she suffered from jaundice. She lightly touched the bruised areas, testing for underlying damage to the bone. It hurt, but didn't feel like anything was crushed.

Someone had braided her hair, but fuzzies stuck up everywhere and her scalp itched. She pulled the band from the tail of the braid and slid it on her wrist. Undoing the braid, she realized she wouldn't be able to put it back up with only one arm. Oh well, she could ask whoever braided it the first time to put it back up for her.

Another knock. "Miss France?"

Jeez, she was impatient. "I'm coming." Maybe this woman, whoever she was, could fill in some of the gaps. Her stomach growled. And provide food.

Emme opened the door and was greeted by an older woman wearing a hijab loosely wrapped around her head an neck.

The Middle East then. Or still Europe, but someone of the Muslim faith.

She stood with her hands clasped in front of her and a pleasant smile. "Good afternoon, Miss France. I'm Fatima, your nurse. How are you feeling?"

Good question. She didn't really hurt. Achy, maybe. "Weak. Hungry. Dirty. Confused."

Fatima's wide smile displayed a tiny dimple under the corner of her bottom lip. "I believe I can help with some of those things." She angled her body and indicated a padded bench at the foot of the bed. "If you would care to sit, I can pull your hair back for you."

Emme ducked her head and ran a hand over her hair. "Sorry. It was sticking up all over the place."

"That's quite all right. I'll pull it back in a bun. I can help you wash it after you eat."

A bath would be heaven. Maybe two. One to wash the funk off

and another to soak in. "Thank you." She eased onto the end of the bench and Fatima pulled her hair away from her face.

"Where am I?"

"Abu Dhabi."

One correct guess. "How did I get here?"

"I'm afraid I don't know that. Dr. Tuska hired me after you were already here."

Her fingers on her scalp felt wonderful. "Who is Dr. Tuska?"

Fatima finished her hair and stepped in front of her. "I don't think I can answer all the questions you have. If you will settle back in bed, I will order room service and let Major Grant know you are awake."

Major Grant? Her brow wrinkled, but she nodded. "We're in a hotel?"

"Yes." Fatima straightened the bed covers and fluffed the pillows. "What would you like to eat?"

She bit her lip. She'd dreamed of a huge stack of buttermilk pancakes smothered in syrup while she'd been counting grains of rice, but her stomach probably wouldn't handle that so well. "A cheese omelet? And fruit, please."

"Of course." She gestured toward the bed and Emme climbed in. Fatima pulled the sheets up to her waist.

Settling against the pillows, exhaustion pressed down on her.

"I'll let Major Grant know you are awake."

"Thank you." She might not be for much longer. Her eyelids grew heavy. That little bit of activity had drained her. The door pushed open.

Jordan. "I thought I dreamed you." Her gaze roamed his face. She hadn't seen him in more than a decade, but she would have recognized him anywhere. There was no mistaking those green eyes and dimpled chin. She'd called it his face butt when they'd been kids. No way she'd call him that now. He was even better looking now than he'd been when she was a teenager with a crush. The plain blue t-shirt fit tight across his shoulders and chest, showing off his muscles.

Oh my god. Jordan Grant is in a bedroom with me and I'm disgusting.

He sat on the edge of the bed. "No dream, slugger. How're you feeling?"

Embarrassed! "Sore. Hungry."

He smiled, showing off his perfect white teeth. A bath was going to be the first order of business. "Fatima was ordering from room service when I came in."

She nodded. "What happened?"

He shifted on the bed and pressed his hip into hers. "How much do you remember?"

"Everything up to the explosion."

He nodded. His gaze moved to her cheek and his face grew tight, but he explained how her father had hired Jared Westin and Titan. She smiled. He probably hadn't found them in the back of *Soldier of Fortune*.

"What about Abu Dhabi? How did we get here?"

"Airplane," he said, straight-faced.

"Jackass." She forgotten how dry his sense of humor was. "Why here and not back home?"

"Ah. See, that question makes more sense. Jared and your father—"

"I have your food, Miss France," Fatima said from the door.

She tried to push up with her good arm, but struggled, unable to get her nightgown from under her enough to scoot upright.

Jordan stood. "Lean forward." He grabbed a bolster from the chair beside the bed and put it behind her lower back.

"Thank you." God, she hated feeling helpless. She needed her arm unwrapped so she could take care of herself.

"No problem." He shoved his hands into the pockets of his cargo shorts and stepped to the side. "Do you want me to leave while you eat?

Fatima set the tray on her lap. "No, finish explaining how we got here." She picked up the fork with her left hand and tried to cut the omelet, but it tore into large chunk. She didn't have the dexterity to hold the fork properly. Maybe she could spear the fruit since it was already sliced. Biting a piece of mango, she closed her eyes as the fresh flavor exploded on her tongue. So good.

She opened her eyes to find Jordan staring and Fatima smiling at her. "What?"

"It's good to see you have an appetite," Fatima said. "Can I bring you anything else?"

Emme looked at her tray. "No, thank you. This is perfect."

Fatima bowed her head and left. Jordan remained standing, the same strange look on his face. Why were his eyes pinchy?

"Sit." She pointed her fork at the chair. "You're making me nervous."

He dragged the chair closer to the bed and propped one foot over the other knee.

"Finish what you were saying," she said around a piece of pineapple.

"Right. Your dad and Jared decided you should recuperate here for a couple of weeks before traveling back to the States."

"Why?

He sighed and ran a hand over his head. "The media got wind of your rescue and has been spinning up a storm. They're camped out at your parents' and brother's houses. It was expected. This way you can heal and give the media time to get distracted with the next celebrity divorce."

She nodded. "Are my parents coming here?"

"No," he said, slowly. He took a small breath. "I'm staying with you until it's time to go back."

Swallowing hard around the lump that formed in her throat, she looked at the tray. "Can I call them?" She hated that her voice was small, but she wanted her mom and dad.

He leaned forward and put his hand on her leg. "Hey. Of course, as soon as you're finished eating. Jared has a VTC set up, so you can see and talk to them. Okay?"

She nodded. "How long have we been here?" She missed the comforting weight of his hand when he leaned back in the chair.

"We landed early this morning. Why aren't you eating your omelet?"

Her cheeks warmed and she turned the fork in her fingers. "I can't cut it without making a mess, so I'm waiting until you're gone."

He reached over and took the fork from her. She watched his long fingers as they maneuvered the fork, cutting the omelet into bite-sized pieces. She'd always had a thing for hands. What would they feel like on her skin?

Holy cow, she needed to get a grip. She was an invalid, for crying out loud. A dirty one at that. Not that he would ever look at her as anything more than Doug's little sister anyway.

He handed her the fork.

"Thank you."

"Welcome." He sat back and propped his foot up again.

She shoveled some egg onto her fork, but paused with it halfway to her mouth. "How are you here? I thought you were still in the Army." The egg fell off the fork. Frick.

"I am."

Managing to get some egg in her mouth, she made a 'continue' motion with the fork.

"Jared Westin has a lot of connections and he pulled some strings to get me on the mission."

"But why you?"

He ran his hand over his head. Did he always do that when he was uncomfortable with something? "Your mom wanted someone you'd know when you were rescued."

That sounded exactly like her mom. All of a sudden her appetite was gone and she set her fork down. "I've had enough.

Can we call them now?"

"Of course. Let me go get the laptop." He was halfway across the room before he returned to the bed. "Are you really finished eating, or do you just want to talk to your parents."

She stared at her half-eaten food. "I'm done."

He picked up the tray and left the room, leaving the door open behind him. The murmur of deep male voices reached her, but she couldn't see who was talking.

One blink. Two. Her eyes fell closed. Images flashed through her mind, discordant and out of sequence. Except the last one. The fist swinging toward her face. "No!" Her eyes flew open and she threw up her good arm to protect herself from the figure looming over her.

"Emme. Emme. It's me. You're safe." He set the laptop on the bedside table. "You're safe, Emme. No one is hurting you."

Her breaths came in gasps, her chest heaving with each inhale as she struggled to separate the memory from reality.

Jordan. Rescue. Abu Dhabi. She'd only dozed off for a minute, maybe two.

He sat back in the chair and leaned forward, elbows on his knees, brows pinched together. "Do you want to wait to call your parents?" His voice was low and soft, his concern evident.

She wiped away the tears on her cheeks and took several bracing breaths. "No. I want to talk to them now. I need to talk to them."

"Okay." He picked up the laptop, flipping open the top.

Electronic ringing came from the speakers and then her father's voice. "Jordan. How is she?"

"She's awake, sir. She's waiting to speak to you."

"Lori!" her father yelled. She smiled. Her mom was probably in the next room.

"For goodness sakes, Emmard. Stop yelling. What is it? Oh, hello, Jordan. Is there any update?

"Yes, ma'am. Just a minute." He turned the laptop and placed in on her lap.

She adjusted the screen to get rid of the reflection. Not that she could see through her tears. "Hi, Daddy. Hi, Mama." A sob escaped. She clapped her hand over her mouth. At that moment, she wasn't an independent thirty-something woman. She was a little girl who wanted to be wrapped in the safe arms of her parents.

Her mom cried. "Oh, baby. Look at your face."

Her dad wrapped his arm around her mother and pulled her into the pocket of his shoulder.

She never realized how much that simple move, one she'd seen them do throughout her life, summed up her parents and everything she wanted for herself. To feel safe, protected, and loved.

Her father kept his military bearing, but she could see the shimmer in his eyes. "Baby girl, you holding up?"

"Yes, Daddy," she whispered. She could be eighty years old and he would still be her daddy.

"Those Titan boys taking care of you?" Her mom turned her head so she was looking at the camera again.

Emme smiled at Jordan and a group of special forces guys being called boys. "Yes. They're taking care of me." Jordan stood and walked into the bathroom, returning with a box of tissues. She took them with a smile.

"Good. Good. You'll be home soon, Emme," her dad said.

She wiped at her eyes. "I know. I just wish I was there now."

"We do too, sweetie," her mom said. "But it's better this way. You can recover without all the reporters banging on your door at all hours of the day."

"Is that really happening?"

"Freaking leeches, every single one of them," her dad said. "We gave 'em a freaking statement. No freaking comment."

"It'll die down soon and they'll move on to the next big story."

"Doesn't help that doctor friend of yours keeps talking to every two-bit hack with a microphone," her dad said.

Emme shook her head. "What doctor friend?"

Her mom patted her dad on the chest. "The British one, sweetie."

"Bennedict?"

"Yes, that one."

"Fancy-pants, prissy name if you ask me."

Jordan coughed into his hand and she glared at him. "Why is he talking to the press?"

Her mom tried to speak, but her father was on a roll. "Who the hell knows. Looking to cash in on his fifteen-minutes of fame. Not that he should be cashing in on anything. He wasn't the one who was kidnapped and beaten."

"Emmard," her mom admonished.

"Jackass," he mumbled.

Emme smiled. "It'll blow over, Dad. How're Doug and Gilly?"

"They're good." Her mom beamed. "They're going to have a baby!"

She gasped. "I'm going to be an aunt?"

"I'm going to be a grandmother!" Her mom bounced and her dad dropped his arm. "We can go shopping for the baby stuff when you get home."

"Jeez, you have months to get things for the baby," her dad said.

"We're not buying everything at once, Emmard. We can get some of the basics now."

She smiled as her parents bickered, then let out a huge yawn.

"Oh, honey. We're sorry." Concern played across her mom's face. "You need your rest. We'll let you go. We can talk again tomorrow. Doug and Gilly are coming over for lunch, so we'll see if we can get the time right and call when they're here."

She yawned again. "Okay. I have no idea what the time difference is. Or what day it is."

"It's Saturday evening here," Jordan said. He raised his voice. "Just let us know what time."

"We'll tell them to come a little early so we can call before it gets too late there," her mom said. "We love you, Emme."

Another tear fell. "Love you too, Mama."

"Same here, baby girl."

"Love you, Daddy."

Her mom blew kisses while her dad reached toward the camera. The screen went dark and she dropped back onto the pillows.

Jordan took the laptop, closed it, and set it on the table. "You okay?"

She shook her head. She'd never missed home so bad in her life. Not since her first semester at college. The bed moved and she raised her head. Jordan took the bolster from behind her neck and slid his arm under her head. He pulled her into his arms and the floodgates opened. She soaked his shirt.

His hand smoothed up and down her back. For the first time in weeks she was safe and protected. Maybe if she didn't think about it too hard, she could pretend the person holding her did it out of love as well.

CHAPTER 8

She'd fallen asleep almost an hour ago and he stayed right where he was. Damn, she felt right in his arms. What the fuck was he doing? He'd known almost to the moment she fell asleep, her head tucked under his chin. Her tears had nearly killed him. Fuck. He'd wanted to go back to Mali and kill those fuckers all over again.

No family should ever have to go through that. She'd put on a brave face for her parents, as if she hadn't been living through her own personal hell. He couldn't help but admire her strength.

He tucked a strand of hair behind her ear. Fuck. He needed to get out of her bed.

Loosening his hold, he slid his arm out from under her neck and eased from the bed. He grabbed the laptop and left the door cracked behind him.

"How's your girl?" Westin asked. He shoved a piece of steak into this mouth.

Jordan shook his head. "She's out. Don't suppose you ordered one for me." Westin pointed toward the dining table and a covered plate. He grabbed the plate, napkin, and silverware and sat down on the plush love-seat. He opened the laptop on the coffee table. "Have you been watching any of the news about her? Us?"

Westin drank some beer before answering. "There haven't been that many reports on it here. One or two on BBC. Parker's monitoring feeds back home. Why?"

Jordan stared at the beer, then Westin. "We're in a Muslim country. Where did you get beer?"

"The fridge."

"No shit." He went to the small fridge and opened it. "Where the hell did you get Sam Adams?"

"It's Abu Dhabi. It's the Las Vegas of the Middle East."

He popped the cap and rejoined Westin. "I thought that was Dubai."

He shrugged. "They're about the same."

Cutting into the perfectly cooked steak, he chewed and pulled up a search engine on the computer.

"You looking up news about Emme?"

He typed out his search and hit enter. "Her parents mentioned a doctor who's been making statements in the news."

"That guy. What a fuckwad."

Jordan stabbed the green beans. "What's he been saying."

"Not a lot, honestly. Just the way he says it makes me want to throat punch him. He's been on every talk show and news channel possible in the last two days."

"What's his story?"

"Parker's looking into it."

He nodded and clicked on the first link. The video showed a slender, dark-haired man. *"Emmeline France is a dedicated medical professional. She's a very special woman and I hope she is safe, wherever she is."*

"They're all like that. He's worried about where she is. No one is claiming responsibility for her rescue. That sort of bullshit."

Jordan's forehead wrinkled. "Who is he?"

"Doctor at the NGO your girl worked for. Parker's digging

deeper. Emme can fill us in tomorrow if she's up to it." He got up and took his empty plate to the dining room table. "We're running in the morning. You in?"

"Yeah, sure."

"Later."

"Later." Jordan ate while clicking through links of news reports on Emme's kidnapping and interviews the doctor had given. Westin was right. He wanted to throat punch the fucker. Something about him was off.

He looked over his shoulder at Emme's room. Who was this guy to her? He closed the laptop, put it on the side table, and plugged it in.

Standing outside Emme's room, he hesitated. Should he check on her? He'd left her less than an hour ago. Would he've heard her if she'd woken up? What if she was having another nightmare and wasn't crying out? He'd been stuck in those dreams, screaming in his head, but not making a sound while he slept.

Screw it. They were all excuses to watch her sleep. Pushing open the door, the light from the living room spilled across the foot of the bed. Enough light reached in that he could see her lying on her back. Her hair had fallen out of its bun and spilled across the pillow.

He was fucked.

He stepped back and pulled the door closed again. He needed his head checked. She wasn't his girl and he needed to remember that.

~

Still trying to catch his breath, Jordan inserted his key into the lock of the hotel door and pushed it open. He guzzled the last of his water and crushed the bottle as he walked into the suite. Hell, it wasn't even that. It was a goddamned penthouse apartment in one of the most expensive hotels in Abu

Dhabi. He shook his head in disbelief for the umpteenth time since they'd arrived. Private security sure as hell paid well.

He stopped dead in his tracks as Emme left the bedroom dressed in tight fitting jeans and a blousy, long-sleeved shirt. A large sling held her arm close to her body.

"Hey."

He swallowed hard. "Hey. How do you feel?"

"Human." She toyed with the end of her braid. "Fatima helped me wash my hair."

Had helping been an option? "Oh. Have you eaten yet?"

"A little while ago, after Dr. Tuska left."

He nodded at her shoulder. "He fit you with the sling?"

She looked down at her arm. "Yes. I have to wear it for a least two weeks, but I shouldn't need surgery."

She was adorable when she scrunched her nose like that.

"Why are you smiling?"

He tried to hide his smile at her accusatory tone. "I just remember, as a kid, you always scrunched your nose whenever you didn't like something."

"That was usually because you and Doug were doing something gross."

"We were boys. Everything we did was gross."

"Exactly." She walked past him and he caught a whiff of the soap she'd used. Something soft and floral. He'd never been one for perfume, but somehow he always seemed to notice her scent. "What's the plan for today?"

Shit. He'd tried to talk Westin out of this on their run. Give Emme a few more days to recuperate. He took a deep breath. "Jared wants to ask you some questions about what happened."

She handed him a cold bottle of water and pulled another one out from the crook of her elbow in the sling. "Okay."

"Okay? That's it?"

"Sure."

He played with the bottle cap. "You good to talk about it?"

She shrugged her good shoulder. "Won't know till we try."

He took a drink of water. Was she being too blasé about the whole thing? She was holding up better than some guys he knew. Or appeared be, at least.

"Are you going to shower?" she asked.

"What?"

"Shower. That thing that has pipes that brings water up through the wall and releases it in a spray. Although my shower has steam too. It was awesome."

Do not think about her naked in the shower. Do not think about her... Too late. "I see someone flipped their sarcasm switch to on." He angled his body away from her and headed to the bedroom on the other side of the suite.

"Just trying to be helpful. You seemed confused," she called after him.

He grinned. Damn, she was sassy. "Jared will be here in less than an hour."

"Okay."

Fuck he was hard. The black silkies did nothing to hide his raging erection. So much for running out some of his frustration. Ten miles should've done it with the brutal paced they'd set. Instead, trading quips with Emme had energized him.

He stripped out of his clothes and stepped into the shower, turning the knob to lukewarm. He'd never been a fan of cold showers — for any reason. Pouring shampoo into his hand, he lathered his short hair, then ran his hands over his chest and abs. He gripped his shaft, stroking from the base to the head in one long stroke, pulling when he reached the tip.

Emme in those jeans. Hugging her hips and lush ass. She'd filled out in all the right places. He'd wanted to drop to his knees and worship her body. Run his tongue from her belly to the junction of her thighs. Feel her hot center against his mouth.

Closing his eyes, he braced his hand against the tiled wall of the shower and let the water cascade down his neck and back.

Firm, long strokes.

Would she scream when she came? Or go breathless? Scrape her nails along his scalp or dig them into his shoulder? He'd throw one of her legs over his shoulder and bury his face in her hot pussy.

Short, fast strokes.

Hold her up until she came all over his face, then lay her down on the floor and keep going until she begged for him to stop.

The base of his spine tingled and his balls grew tight. He grit his teeth together and groaned as he came.

Jesus. He might not make it two weeks.

~

*D*amn, he was hot. She sat on the end of the bed and fell back, staring up at the ceiling. It should be illegal for a guy to walk around looking like that. Tight, sweaty, t-shirt molded to his chest and abs. Short, black shorts showing off strong, muscular thighs. She followed pages on Facebook dedicated to guys like that. Man candy. He could have his own page and get a bazillion likes.

There had to be something wrong with her. She had fading bruises on her face and her shoulder was in a sling, but her libido was still going strong. Yay hormones.

Maybe it was a physiological, evolutionary response to propagating the species in the face of imminent danger. How would a study like that be conducted? Here, let me almost kill you and see if you want to have sex afterwards. Could she get funding for a study like that? Better question, could she get Jordan to volunteer?

Knock. Knock. "Emme?"

"Yeah."

"You okay?"

Does imagining you naked count as okay? "Yes, just resting a bit."

"Jared and the rest of the guys are here. You up for talking to them?"

She pushed up on the bed and sighed. "I'm coming." She padded across the room and went out into the suite.

Nope. No. She was going back in her room and not leaving it until the ugly guys showed up. Where did this company recruit from? Hot-Guys-R-Us?

Jordan took her good elbow and led her to the sitting area. "Emme, this is Jared Westin, owner of Titan Group. Colby Winters and Cash Garrison, two of the other guys that were on the rescue mission."

These were the guys who rescued her. Her heroes. She threw herself at Jared and wrapped her good arm around his waist. "Thank you."

"It was our pleasure, sweetheart." He returned her hug. She buried her head in his shoulder as the tears welled up. He held her gently for a several minutes until she calmed down. "You ready to talk?"

She nodded and pulled away. That was embarrassing. "Sorry. I seem to be crying at the drop of a hat these days."

"That's understandable. It'll probably last a few more," Cash said.

A tissue appeared in front of her and she wiped at her eyes. "Thanks."

Jordan pulled her down onto the small couch and sat close, the hard muscles of his leg pressed against her.

Jared sat across from them on them the sofa. Cash sat in the chair facing the room while Colby took one of the bar stools. Did they create the barrier around her on purpose or was it inherent to their training?

"Emme, what do you remember about your kidnapping?" Jared asked.

She took a deep breath and clenched the tissue in her hand. It was hard, walking them through the last few weeks, from the moment the gunmen barged into the clinic until the moment Titan rescued her. Describing the beatings was the worst and she had to stop more than once. They were patient with her, giving her the time to gather herself and keep going.

Jordan's hand was warm in hers. Had she taken his or had he taken hers? It didn't matter. She drew strength from his strong grip.

"Did you see anyone other than your captors?" Jared asked.

"No. Only Anuli. I didn't even see the other two women that were taken." She caught the look Jared gave Jordan. "Why?"

Jared leaned forward, propped his elbows on his knees, and clasped his hands. "We thought you had been targeted because of your blog."

"My blog?" No one read her blog. She barely got a dozen hits a day. "Why?"

"You talked about a lot of unpopular topics. Especially in that region of the world."

"But you don't think that now."

"You were targeted, but not because of your blog."

"Then why?"

"Did you apply or were you recruited by the NGO?"

"A little of both, I guess. One of the nurses or doctors at the hospital I was working at mentioned it, I think, and I looked into it. What does this have to do with why I was targeted?"

"Was the doctor Bennedict Wormwell?"

"It's possible." Silence stretched out for several seconds. "Can you please cut to the chase and tell me what this is about?"

Jordan let out a bark of laughter and smirked at Jared. "Glad to see it I'm not the only one bothered by your lack of words."

Jared sat back in the couch. "You're not the first doctor to be taken hostage for ransom in the region. Four other doctors in the last three years have been kidnapped. All four had a connection to Bennedict Wormwell."

No, that wasn't possible. "Bennedict might be a smarmy ass,

but he couldn't be involved in an international kidnap-for-ransom scheme." She scoffed. "That stuff only happens in movies."

"All the kidnappings happened in Western Africa. All the victims were pretty doctors or nurses. All employed in some capacity by Medical Relief United. All were recruited by Dr. Wormwell and all had some sort of relationship with him."

She shook her head. "That has to be coincidence." It couldn't be possible. Right?

Jared never broke eye contact. "We traced the money to him, Emme."

She stared at him while it sank in. "That mother fucker."

Colby coughed into his hand and Jared cracked a grin.

Glad they found it amusing.

Jordan squeezed her hand. "What was your relationship with him?"

And things were awkward. "Uh."

"I need to know, Emme." Jared said. "I need to know how he's getting close to his targets."

"We had a brief fling."

"How brief?" Jordan asked. There was an edge to his voice and his face tensed when she looked at him.

"Very brief."

"Who broke it off?" Jared asked.

She looked at him. "I did. Not that there was really anything to break off. We weren't dating or anything."

"Why did you break it off?" Jordan asked.

She shifted on the couch. This was stuff she talked to her girlfriends about, not souped-up, alpha-males who had more testosterone than a professional football team. She dropped her head onto the cushion and looked up at the ceiling. "Does it matter?"

"It might," Jared said. His voice was a weird combination of soft and hard. As if he expected some cataclysmic event had led to her breaking things off with Bennedict.

She raised her head. They asked for it. "He had a small dick and sucked in bed."

Colby started choking and almost fell of the stool. Jared ran a hand over his face, but she could tell he was doing it to hide his smile. She was afraid to look and see Jordan's reaction.

"What are you going to do with all this information?"

"We'll take care of it," Cash said. "We don't take well to people who take advantage of women."

"Take care of it like, 'make him sleep with the fishes' take care of it?"

Cash grinned. "Who do you think we are?"

"Uh, the guys who invaded Mali, blew up a building, and rescued me." She shook her head. It wasn't out of the realm of possibilities that they'd kill Bennedict. It might make her blood-thirsty, but she wouldn't mind seeing him bleed a little. Who the hell worked with terrorists and kidnapped doctors? It made her blood boil now that she thought about it.

"We'll make sure the right people are made aware of what's going on." Jared stood. "We're leaving tomorrow."

Her brow furrowed. "I thought we were going to be here for a couple of weeks?"

"You and Jordan will be. We," he indicated Colby and Cash, "are going home tomorrow. Someone from the embassy will be here sometime next week with your passports."

"Really?" she asked. "How are you managing that?"

"I called in a favor," Jared said.

"Jared has a lot of strings," Jordan said.

"He's a goddamn puppet master," Cash said, earning a glare from Jared. "Am I wrong?"

"You're not wrong," Colby said. "Modern day Geppetto."

Jared turned his glare to Colby. "Assholes."

She smiled.

Jared came around the low table and held out a hand. Emme stood and took it. "Call the concierge if you need anything while you're here. I know you want to be home, but it's good to let things die down."

She nodded. "I know. Thank you. For everything. For…you know."

"It's what we do. Take care of yourself."

She nodded. If she said anything else, she'd probably lose it again. Colby and Cash said their goodbyes, pulling her in for a hug and telling her to take care.

Then they were gone. And she was alone. With Jordan.

CHAPTER 9

*H*e watched her walk from the windows to the bar, grab a water and set it down, just to repeat the motion.

"Do you want to go for a walk?" he asked.

She turned, the light from the windows behind her accenting her curves. "What?"

He fought the urge to adjust himself. "A walk? On the beach. We're only about a hundred yards or so from the promenade."

Damn, he felt her smile in his dick. She had one tooth that slightly overlapped another. It didn't detract from her beauty, but kept her from being too perfect. Was that a thing? Too perfect?

"Did you just say 'promenade'?"

His eyebrows rose. "Isn't that what it's called?"

"Well, yeah. I'm just surprised you know that."

"Because I'm a dumb G.I.?"

"No, 'cause you're a guy period. That's not normally a word a guy uses. Especially a guy who's all," she bowed up her free arm and tucked her chin in, "grrr."

He grinned. "A bear?"

She dropped her arm and stood straight. "Not a bear. A, you know, manly-man."

He ran a hand down his abs. "You think I'm manly?"

She rolled her eyes. "I'm not feeding any more of your ego."

He pulled his shoulders back and puffed out his chest. "I think you're evading the question."

"I'm evading giving you a big head." She walked over to the couch and sat down. "I can't go for a walk anyway."

Shit. Was she in pain? Did the doc leave anything for her? "Does something hurt? Do I need to call Fatima?"

"No, the painkillers are working fine. I don't have any shoes." She stretched her legs out in front of her and wiggled her toes.

The tension in his shoulders released. "Oh. Where did you get the clothes?"

"Fatima said to help myself to what was in the closet."

"No shoes?"

She shook her head. "Not in my size."

"Stand by." He picked up the phone on the side table and pressed zero.

"Good morning, concierge."

"Good morning. Is it possible to have someone purchase some shoes?"

"Of course, sir. What type of shoes?"

He drew a blank. "Hang on a sec." He pulled the phone away from his ear and looked at Emme, who had stretched out on the couch. "What kind of shoes?"

"Comfortable walking shoes. Size eight. And socks."

He repeated her request to the concierge.

"We will send a selection up to your room shortly."

"Thank you."

Emme had propped her head on the armrest. Her eyes were closed and her hand rested under her cheek. The opening of her shirt had gaped, exposing her deep cleavage. Well, fuck. Now what? He paced around the room.

The walk was supposed to be a distraction. Something to keep them occupied now that they were alone. In a suite. With three large beds in close proximity.

Quit thinking about the beds, asshole.

Dropping to the floor on the far side of the room, he knocked out a few dozen pushups. Had to keep up his manly physique. He smirked. She thought he was hot. He flipped over to do sit-ups.

He needed to figure out a plan for the next two weeks. He'd go nucking futs if he didn't have anything to do. It hadn't even been two hours and he was ready to crawl out of his skin.

Propping his elbows on his knees, he looked at his watch and calculated the time difference. Unless there'd been a delay, his unit should've arrived in Djibouti. They'd be doing a turn-over with the out-going unit. Settling in to their new routine and bitching about the jet lag, lack of space, and crap food.

He rubbed his hands over his head. Getting to his unit once he got Emme home was going to be a pain in the ass. He'd email the sergeant major later and check in to start making arrangements.

A knock sounded at the door and he popped up to answer. Emme sat up on the couch and stretched her arm over her head. She looked at him over her shoulder with sleepy eyes.

He looked through the peephole, opened the door, and stepped back while two men dressed in the hotel uniform and loaded down with shoe boxes entered.

"Good afternoon, sir. Where may we leave these?" one of the men asked.

"The dining table, I guess."

"Very good." They set the boxes on the table, bowed, and left.

There were sixteen boxes on the table.

Emme's blouse brushed his arm when she joined him. Tingles shot through his body and swirled around in his gut and chest. What the fuck was happening to him? He was acting like a teenager getting close to his first crush.

"That's a lot of shoes," she said. "What did you ask for?"

Bemused, he looked at her. She was staring, wide-eyed, at the stack. "Walking shoes. Size eight."

"These are all designer."

He dropped an arm around her shoulders. "Babe. I have no idea what that means."

She looked up at him, the top of her head barely reaching his chin. "It means they're expensive."

He shrugged. "I'm ninety-nine percent sure Titan is paying."

"Huh. Remind me to hug Jared again."

Not fucking likely.

She reached forward and lifted the lid off one of the boxes, pulling out a pair of red, strappy heels. "These are not walking shoes."

No, but they're 'fuck-me' shoes. He pulled his arm from her shoulder. Jesus. He needed to scrub his brain clean and quit thinking about her like that. Sucked for him that she'd burrowed under his skin at some point over the last few days. The more he scratched the worse it itched. Like a chigger.

Lifting the boxes, she looked at the labels on the end. She went through half a dozen boxes before opening one and pulled out a pair of cream canvas flats. Dropping them on the floor, she slipped her feet in and walked across the room, turned, and walked back.

"These'll work," she said.

"You ready? We can find somewhere to eat."

"Let me grab something real quick." She went into her room and returned wearing a gauzy pink scarf draped around her head and neck.

"Why are you wearing that?" he asked.

"We're in a Muslim country." Her tone said *duh.*

"We're not in Saudi. I think you'll be okay."

"It's respectful," she said.

He shrugged. If she wanted to cover her head, he wasn't going to argue. Grabbing the key from the slot on the wall, he held the door open for her.

She stepped out of the suite. "I don't have any money."

"It's covered." He closed the door and headed to the bank of elevators at the end of the hall.

"I don't have any ID, either," she said.

He pushed the down button and smiled at her. "Don't get arrested."

She glared.

He grinned.

The elevator dinged and they entered the car. It stopped halfway down and two men dressed in traditional dishdashas boarded. The assholes gave Emme a once over.

Jordan moved her closer to the corner and stood in front of her, blocking her from view. He folded his arms across his chest and glared at the backs of the two men, daring them to look at her. The doors opened on the ground floor and he waited for the men to exit ahead of them before reaching for Emme's hand.

"That was a very impressive display of manliness. My virtue is suitably defended."

He glared at her. "They shouldn't have been staring."

"Oh, please. That was mild compared to some of the things that've happened back home."

"They were out of line."

"Jordan." She stopped and pulled her hand out of his.

He immediately missed having her slender fingers in his. "They were curious. They didn't leer or make any comments. I've been called a bitch because I said 'no, thank you' when a guy told me to smile."

"What the fuck?"

Her head fell back as if praying for patience and she set her hand on her hip. He braced for the display of temper he knew was coming. Emme had never been one to hold back when they were younger. *This should be good.*

Instead, she dropped her hand and turned in a slow circle, her face alight with wonder. "Oh my god," she whispered.

Sweet baby Jesus, his dick throbbed at the tone of her voice. An image flashed through his mind — Emme spread out under him, writhing and moaning those same words while he was buried balls deep.

Two weeks. *Fuck.*

He looked up, trying to figure out what held her in thrall. "What?" His voice had a bite he didn't intend.

She stopped spinning. "The ceiling."

He looked back up. In the center of the lobby, the ceiling arched up several stories, creating a rough dome of marble. "What about it?"

Her head snapped up. "Seriously? It's beautiful."

He shrugged. "If you say so."

Her mouth opened and closed twice. "If I— Look at it. It's a work of art."

The corner of his mouth tipped up at her outrage. "I'm an Army guy, Emme. Architecture isn't my area of expertise. I'll take your word for it."

She huffed. "Which way?"

He cocked his head to the rear of the foyer and the large hall leading to the back of the hotel. "That way."

Turning on her heel, she walked ahead of him. Her annoyance added an extra flounce to her step and sway in her hips that drew his eyes to her ass. Maybe he shouldn't fault those two men for checking her out.

They exited onto the large flagstone patio and she kept going until she reached the steps leading down to the promenade. Her rib cage expanded slowly. He could see her inhale. She released her breath and repeated the sequence.

He stopped to her right. Her face was tilted up to the sun and her eyes were closed. "You okay?"

"I didn't realize how much I needed this." Her voice was soft and reverent.

His brow furrowed. "What?"

She opened her eyes and looked at him, her eyes sparkling. "The end of the world."

He shook his head. "I don't understand."

"It was really hard at times to remember there was more than that dirt room and getting beat almost every day." Her voice was soft. "My world had become so small and confined. I'd forgotten there was more to it."

"And the ocean helped you remember?"

"Yes."

He tried to see it the way she did. To him it was a natural progression of geography. He turned to face her fully "Did you turn into a hippie?"

Her laugh was surprisingly light and it hit him like a concussive blast. The force of it should have knocked him off his feet and sent him flying. Her ability to laugh like that in the face of everything that had happened floored him.

An unexpected longing filled him. He wanted an eternity to make her laugh like that and to wake up each day with the prospect of being surrounded by happiness and joy.

~

*J*ordan looked like he'd been punched in the gut. Or someone had told him they'd kicked his puppy. Emme touched his arm above the elbow and his muscles jumped under her fingers. Because of her? "Are you okay?"

He gave a slight shake of his head. "Yeah." He shifted to the side and her hand fell away. "Yeah. You hungry? We passed a cafe this morning during our run."

"Sure."

He gestured down the steps to the right and she led the way, waiting for him at the bottom. They followed the walkway from the hotel to the wide path that ran along the low wall separating the beach from the hotels and shops.

Walking beside him in silence was awkward. They were close enough to touch, her arm kept brushing his, but it seemed like he'd put a physical distance between them.

Several minutes passed. Looked like she was going to have to start the conversation. "How long were you in the Army?"

"Still am. I commissioned right out of college."

Her brow wrinkled. "Are you Reserve?"

"No. Active."

"I thought you were with Titan."

"Nope."

Can I get a three-syllable word, Pat? She stopped. "How does that work?"

He turned back and slipped his hands into the pockets of his khakis, pulling them further down on his hips. "Didn't I explain that?"

"You said Dad hired Titan. I assumed he hired Titan because of you."

"Ah, no. It was the other way around. Your mom wanted someone on the mission that you had some familiarity with. I don't think she wanted you here by yourself or with a complete stranger. So your dad pulled some strings and got me put on special orders."

Her mouth quirked. "Of course he did."

He stepped closer and she swore she could feel the heat from his broad chest.

"They love you, Emme. They just wanted you safe and taken care of."

"I'm not upset," she assured him. "Knowing Dad would do everything in his power to get me, kept me going."

His assessing gaze roved over her face. "Okay."

"Okay. Food?" He nodded and they continued down the path. "Why the Army?"

"Your dad," he said.

"Really?"

"You and Doug always groaned whenever he told his old war stories"

"That's because we'd heard them a bazillion times."

He smiled. "I soaked them up. Whenever Doug and I played soldiers, I always wanted to be your dad. He gave me my recommendation for ROTC."

"Really? I had no idea." Of course, she'd barely been a teenager when he and Doug went off to college. There'd been no reason for her to know. "What do you do?"

"I'm a Ranger." He pointed to a small restaurant a few yards off the path, a dozen or so umbrella covered tables out front.

"Of course you are."

A young Filipino woman greeted them at the door. "Welcome. Two?"

"Yes. Can we sit outside?" Jordan asked.

The hostess nodded and gestured to the tables. They sat next to each other, facing the promenade and ocean, and took the menus.

"Why did you say 'of course you are' like that?" Jordan asked.

"If you hero worshipped Dad, it makes sense you followed in his footsteps." Emme opened her menu. "Plus, there's the whole invading a small African country and blowing it up." She winked over the top of her menu. Her gaze dropped to his smile, now surrounded by reddish-blond scruff.

"It was a wall, not an entire country."

She raised an eyebrow.

"Fine. Two walls."

The waiter arrived at the table and she asked for sparkling water. "Do you know what you want?" she asked when the waiter left.

"What on here is meat?"

She hid her smile behind her menu. "Haven't you been to the Middle East before?"

"Yes, but that did actually involve invading and blowing up countries, not sitting down at restaurants."

"Trust me?" she asked.

He stared at her for a heartbeat, then closed his menu and put it on the table. "Go for it."

She smiled and his gaze dropped to her mouth. Her breath caught and her pulse picked up. Was he as aware of her as she was of him? She licked her lips and his gaze flew back to hers. His green eyes were intense and held a heat she felt in her core.

The waiter set their glasses down on the table and broke the spell. She felt flushed and was tempted to use the menu as a fan.

"Madame?" The waiter asked.

"I'm sorry?" What was the question?

"You were going to order," Jordan reminded her.

"Oh, right." She glanced at him again, but couldn't hold his gaze — it was still too intense. "The shish kabob, tabouleh, and hummus, please."

The waiter bowed and took the menus. Emme sipped the cool water, taking a moment to slow her heart beat. "Where are you stationed?"

"North Carolina."

"Do you like the Army?"

He didn't answer right away. "It was all I ever wanted to do."

Emme set her glass on the table. "You said 'was.'"

Jordan ran both his hands over his head. "What I wanted was a lot more clear when I was younger."

"And now?"

"Now it's about the men and women in my unit. Making sure they have a leader they can trust and look to when the shit hits the fan."

She nodded. Her dad had said pretty much the same thing. It

wasn't about the Army or the mission. It had been about the people in his unit — the people he'd commanded.

"What about you?" Jordan asked. "What made you decide on nursing?"

She took a sip of her water. "My junior year of high school, I volunteered at a hospital in the pediatric ward. It struck me that the vast majority of the caregivers were nurses. The doctors would roll in on rounds, but the nurses did everything. Got to know the families and the kids. Could recite every fact about their patients. Then I met one who was a nurse practitioner. She could do everything a family doctor could do, but she still got to spend time with her patients."

She shrugged and took a sip of water. "I decided that was what I wanted to do."

"You like it," Jordan said.

She smiled. "I love being a nurse." It was the one thing in her life she'd always been sure of.

"And Mali. What made you go there?"

"One of my professors had spent a year in Thailand. She said it was one of the most rewarding experiences of her career." She shrugged. "The opportunity came up and I took it."

He fiddled with his straw. "Was it? Rewarding?"

"Yes. It was also incredibly frustrating."

"Why?"

How to explain in a way he'd understand? "It was hard not to inject my western ideals and morals into their culture. To understand that I was only there for a short time and no matter how much I wanted to change things, it didn't mean what I wanted for them was better."

"What kind of things did you want to change?"

She sighed. "To keep girls in school longer. To teach them a skill to support themselves so they wouldn't have to marry at such a young age. Practice birth control so even if they did have to marry, they wouldn't get pregnant." She shook her head. "Frustrating."

"And the rewarding part?"

"When a girl finishes school and gets accepted to university. The pride I could see in them."

"Are you going to go back?"

"Probably not."

"Why probably?"

"Well, for one, I don't want to go back overseas and put Mom and Dad through worrying about me again. Plus, that seems like a huge slap in the face to you and the guys from Titan. And two, I haven't had time to figure out what I'm going to do. I didn't even have shoes until an hour ago."

She squirmed in her seat. God, when he smiled…everything in her twisted and flipped like an Olympic gymnast.

Their food arrived and Jordan poked at the square chunks of grilled lamb on his plate. "What is it?"

"It's meat. Put it in your mouth."

He coughed and choked on the piece he'd taken. "Jesus, Emme." He took a drink of water. "Warn a guy."

She grinned and scooped tabouleh onto a piece of flat bread. "What about you? What happens for you when we get back to the real world?"

"I catch up with my unit."

"Where are they?"

"Horn of Africa," he said. "This is really good. What is it?"

"Shish." He was deploying in two weeks. She knew enough about world events to know the Horn of Africa was dangerous. It wasn't Iraq, but it wasn't exactly a garden spot either.

"Emme."

Her gaze flew to his. "You're deploying?" Her voice sounded shrill and she cringed inwardly.

"Well, yeah. It's what I do."

"For how long?"

"It'll be close to six months."

"When do you leave?"

He cocked his head and a crease formed between his brows. "As soon as I get back. I need to get in touch with the sergeant major to make arrangements."

The bottom dropped out of her stomach. *It's too soon. I just found him again.*

It felt like something she'd always wanted was slipping through her fingers — again. Her reaction was out of proportion to the situation, but it felt significant. Like a moment in time that could determine the rest of her life.

The backs of his fingers on the side of her neck sent a jolt of longing through her.

"Emme, you're worrying me. Are you hot? Should we go inside?"

She grasped his palm. "No. I'm just surprised they're making you deploy as soon as you get back."

"I need to get back to my guys." His voice was soft.

She got it. She did. That didn't mean she liked it. She gave him a tight smile and pulled his hand away from her neck.

Someone screamed. He struggled against the bonds of sleep, wresting free of the veil that held him down. Sitting up in bed, he cocked his head, listening. Emme'd had nightmares the last two nights, but she'd woken herself each time. She'd been strong when telling Westin about everything that had happened, but he hated that she was reliving it in her sleep. If hers were anything like his own nightmares, they would be bad.

There it was again. Slightly muffled, followed by an anguished sob coming from across the suite. He pushed back the covers and grabbed the t-shirt from the end of the bed, pulling it over his head. He jogged across the suite and he stood just outside her door. She'd left it cracked and he listened. Another cry and he eased through the door.

She lay on one side of the huge bed, tangled in sheets. She whimpered and rolled toward the middle of the bed.

Damn, she wasn't waking on her own. He sat on the edge of the bed, careful not to touch her and startle her awake.

"Shhhh shhhh shhhh. It's okay Emme. You're safe."

Her eyes snapped opened and she jerked away from him. "Jordan?"

"Yeah."

"What are you doing here?"

"I heard you scream."

"Oh." She closed her eye and covered her face with her hand. "I'm sorry."

"Emme, you don't need to be sorry. Nightmares are normal. I expected them before now, to be honest."

She sniffled into her pillow.

Shit. What was he supposed to do? "Do you want me to leave?"

She shook her head, still buried in the pillow.

He reached out to touch her, but stopped. "I don't— I don't know what to do, Emme."

"Will you hold me?" Her voice was soft. Unsure.

Shit, it broke his heart.

Lying next to her, he slid an arm under her pillow and gathered her close, trying to be gentle. At his touch, she launched herself at him, burrowing into the crook of his neck. Sobs wracked her body.

Fuck. I think I'd rather be shot at. All he could do was rub her back and make shushing sounds while she cried her eyes out. It worked. Either that or exhaustion took over, but she finally settled into sleep.

His body noticed how well she fit against him. His mind told him to quit being an asshole.

～

The first thing Emme noticed was the steady heartbeat under her ear. The second was the pool of drool under her cheek. So gross. And embarrassing.

She lifted her head. Maybe it would dry before he woke up. Her plan was thwarted when his arms tightened around her. Tilting her head back, she found him looking at her in the predawn light.

"Morning." His voice was gruff and still thick with sleep.

"Morning. I drooled on you."

His smile was almost blinding. He closed his eyes and dropped his head back. "Not the worst thing I've ever been covered in."

Pulling the edge of the sheet up, she wiped at her cheek. "Sorry."

His arm tightened around her briefly. "Gotta stop apologizing, babe. None of this is worth saying sorry for."

"Thank you, then."

He looked back at her. "For what?"

"Staying with me last night." She dropped her gaze. "Rescuing me. I don't think I've said it."

"Think it's one of those things that can go without saying. You doing okay?"

Was she doing okay? Her shoulder ached. Every now and then, her ribs would twinge when she breathed too deeply. Her face was still a patchwork of fading bruises. Physically, she'd heal. But everything else? The mental things? The nightmares and flashbacks? She'd need to talk to someone. But right now... Tears welled up in her eyes.

"Hey. Hey, hey. What's going on? What happened?"

She shook her head and tried to hide her face.

"Emme, talk to me."

"I can't," she whispered. What could she say? She couldn't even explain it to herself.

"Do you want me to leave?"

She moved closer to him and shook her head. That was the last thing she wanted. Jordan made her feel safe. Protected. She knew he wouldn't let anything happen to her. He'd literally fought for her already.

"You're killing me. I don't know what to do." His hands ran up and down her back, trying to sooth her.

"Kiss me." Oh, jeez. Did she really just say that? Is that what she wanted?

"Emme—"

"Please, Jordan." She unburied her head. "I want you to kiss me. I need you to. I need to feel something other than all the crap I'm feeling now."

A small furrow appeared between his brows.

"Please," she whispered.

His head tilted and hovered a hairsbreadth away from her lips. She slid her hand behind his head, running her fingers over the soft stubble at the base of his neck and pulled him closer. His lips were firm but gentle.

She didn't want gentle. She wanted to feel.

She wanted to feel *him*.

Opening her mouth, she touched her tongue to his lips.

His sharp inhale signaled his surprise and he groaned. "Emme."

"More." She pressed her mouth against his again. He reciprocated and his tongue laved her bottom lip before delving into her mouth to tangle with hers. She moaned and pressed closer, closing the distance between their bodies.

Now she realized why he'd kept some space between them. His erection nudged her lower stomach through their pajama bottoms. She threw her leg over his hips, eliciting a deep groan.

He ended their kiss, pressing his forehead against hers. His breathing was harsh. Tortured. "Emme, we have to stop."

"No, we don't." She tried to pull him back to her mouth, but he resisted.

"You've just gone through a horrible experience. I know you're feeling a lot of confusing emotions, but this isn't the way to handle them."

"You don't understand. You might think you do, but you don't. All my power was stripped from me. I was beaten and tossed around like I was trash. I need to feel something good. I need to have hands on me that don't bring me pain."

God, she sounded pathetic. She was begging a man to touch

her. Something she'd promised she'd never do again after Jordan, of all people, made her realize she was better than that.

What was she doing? He was right — this wasn't the way to handle her issues.

Shame washed over her. Tucking her chin, she tried to roll to the edge of the bed. The bathroom was as good a place as any to hide until he went back to his own room.

His arms held her in place. "Don't run. You're vulnerable right now. I don't want to take advantage of you."

Funny, she'd had the same thought. She flattened her palms on his chest, smoothing the thin material of his shirt. "What if I'm taking advantage of you?"

"How could you take advantage of me?"

Peeking up at him through her lashes, she caught the confusion in his eyes. "What if all I am is the damsel in distress and you're my knight in shining armor?"

"I'm feeling a lot of things right now, but knight in shining armor isn't one of them. Do you feel like a damsel in distress?"

"Yes," she whispered. "And that's the problem. I don't want to feel like that." She took a shuddering breath. "I'm sorry. I shouldn't have— You can let me up now."

His hand ran down her lower back, over her butt, and down her thigh — still resting over his hips. She expected him to push her leg off, but he pulled her closer instead pressing his erection against her. It was her turn to groan.

His lips traveled across her face, landing on every cut and bruise he could reach. "I feel like an ass."

"Why?"

"I should do the right thing." His mouth moved down her neck.

"What's the right thing?"

"Let you go. Get out of this bed and walk away."

Her thumb brushed his nipple. "I don't want that."

He nipped at her ear. "I don't either. I want to kiss everything better. Every cut. Every bruise. Everywhere you hurt and everywhere you don't." One of his hands found her breast, lifting and squeezing. "I don't have any protection, so that's all I can do."

"There's a box of condoms in the bedside table."

He lifted his head. "How do you know that?"

She shrugged and averted her eyes, suddenly embarrassed. "I snooped after my bath last night."

"Nothing wrong with snooping." His finger crooked under her chin, forcing her to look at him. "Are you sure this is what you want?"

"Yes. This is what I want. *You're* what I want."

His lips found hers again. So gentle, it made her heart ache. Even if he was only doing this because she asked him, she knew he was going to treat her like the most precious of treasures.

"Tell me if I hurt you," he whispered against her mouth.

"You're not hurting me." She rolled to her back and he followed, propping his weight on his elbows. Her legs opened, letting him settle in the junction of her thighs. Lifting her hips, she told him without words what she wanted. He thrust gently and she inhaled sharply as desire flashed through her.

"Are you okay?" His mouth traveled down her neck, trailing kisses as he moved lower.

"How about if I tell you when I'm not okay?" She gasped when his mouth found her nipple through her shirt. Sparks shot through her body, sending tingles straight to her happy place. He moved to her other breast and gave it the same attention. Fireworks went off inside her.

Endorphins. Residual adrenaline. Jordan. Evolutionary imperative. Whatever it was, her body was on fire in a way it had never been before. His mouth kept moving down and he used his nose to nudge her shirt up over her belly.

He rose up on his knees and hooked his fingers under the hem of her shirt. "Do you want to take this off?"

Nodding, she arched her back, then lifted her torso and arms so he could pull it off. Inch by slow inch he gathered her shirt in his hands. She wasn't sure if he was taking his time with the reveal or giving her time to change her mind. Letting him do it his way, she waited until she was finally free and watched him suck in a breath. She knew she had at least two large bruises on her upper chest and her shoulder was a mishmash of colors from being dislocated.

The rough pads of his fingers traced each mark, his thumb running across her collarbone and shoulder. His mouth and tongue followed as he kept his word to kiss all her hurts.

Her eyes stung at the gentle way he was treating her. She needed to get back to task. Her hands burrowed under his t-shirt. "Your turn. Take this off."

He grabbed the hem and yanked it over his head, sending it sailing in the general direction he'd sent hers. His abs weren't perfect, but they were pretty damn close. A smattering of blonde hair covered his chest and the old-school American traditional tattoos on his chest. Her eyes followed the thin trail that started just below his belly button and disappeared into the waist band of his pajama pants. His hard-on tented the front and she licked her lips.

"Christ. Don't do that."

Her gaze flew up to his. "Do what?"

"Lick your lips while you're staring at my cock. Otherwise, this isn't going to go the way I plan."

She raised her eyebrows. "How do you plan for it to go?"

He gave her a lopsided grin. "You'll see." He lapped at her belly button before nipping at her lower abdomen, above her waist band. Moving lower, he blew hot breath through her pants before grabbing a handful of material at her hips and pulling her pants down her legs.

She panted, praying he wouldn't stop and that she wouldn't embarrass herself by coming as soon as he touched her. His hands pushed her thighs apart and he wedged his shoulders between her legs. Spreading her outer folds with this thumbs, he tongued the hood of her clit.

Her whole body trembled. She pressed her head back into the pillow and bit her lips to keep from moaning.

"Don't hold back, Emme. Give it to me."

He kept her spread as he licked and sucked at her most sensitive parts. The orgasm coiled deep in her belly like a spring wound too tight. One more turn, one small touch, and it would explode. Jordan pressed his tongue hard against her clit and pushed two fingers into her.

Her world shattered and reverberations spread through her body in waves. She fisted the sheets in her hands and bit back a scream while straining against his hold. She wanted to escape and be closer at the same time. Her hips moved in rhythm to the waves of pleasure coursing through her. The pressure of his tongue eased up as her movements became less frenzied, until he barely touched her. All the tension left her body at once. If she could have collapsed, she would have. Good thing she was already lying down.

His hands left her and she heard the drawer of the table open. The bed shifted and she peeled open her eyes to watch him pull his pants off, foil packet gripped in his teeth. Her breathing picked back up at the sight of him.

God, he was beautiful. He tore the foil packet open and rolled the condom over his erection. His body covered hers, his cock nudging her opening.

"Do you want to keep going?"

Her eyes widened. "Kind of late to be asking that, isn't it?"

He shook his head. "It's never too late to ask that. If you've had enough, I'll stop."

She shifted her hips, rubbing her slick opening along his hard length. "What about you?"

Gritting his teeth, he said, "I'll go rub one out in the shower."

Running her hands down his sides, she grabbed his butt and pulled him in tight. "As much as I'd like to watch that, I want to keep going."

He kissed her. Hard and carnal, none of his earlier gentleness evident. She could tell he was still holding back because of her injuries. His tongue swept into her mouth, mimicking the motion of his hips as he entered her.

She wrapped her legs high on his waist, digging her heels into his ass. He surged forward, sinking deep and she contracted around him. He pulled out and pushed back in, setting a steady rhythm. Her hips rocked to match him.

"Oh god, Emme. You feel so good." His breath was harsh and hot on her neck, where his face was tucked. One hand worked its way between her lower back and the bed. He tilted her hips, changing the angle, allowing him to go even deeper.

The spring coiled tight again, slower this time. She concentrated on the feel of him. The push and pull. The rub of his pelvis on her sensitive nub. She buried her head in his shoulder and let out a sob as the spring released again.

Her orgasm set him off. He thrust hard, shortening his strokes until he sank into her and stayed there while his body shuddered. He rolled them to the side, onto her good shoulder, keeping their connection.

She didn't know how long they'd lain there. All she knew was she could feel him still throbbing inside her. Every time, her body would respond with an answering pulse. She whimpered when he withdrew.

"Need to get rid of this." He kissed her before rolling out of the bed and walking into the bathroom.

Emme watched his retreat while her mind raced. Holy cow. She'd just had sex with Jordan. Really good sex. Hire-a-skywriter good sex. She should have listened to him. Should have let him hold her and left it at that. Because she was pretty sure she'd fallen in love with him.

It's just endorphins. The trauma.

Shit. Who was she kidding? She'd been in love with Jordan Grant since she was fifteen years old. She'd been fooling herself for the past decade and a half, telling herself it was a school-girl crush. She probably could have kept up that lie if this hadn't happened, but now she knew the feel of his body in hers. No one had ever measured up to the myth she'd built in her head and now no one would ever be able to live up to the reality.

He came back into the room and she cursed herself for not taking the time to put her clothes back on. He didn't seem to have an issue with it since he climbed back into the bed with her. He folded an arm under his head and lay on his back next to her, staring at the ceiling.

"What are you thinking about?" he asked.

She smiled. "Isn't that supposed to be my line?"

He turned his head and smirked. "I forgot how sarcastic you could be. No regrets?"

Was he unsure himself? "No. Absolutely no regrets."

Nodding, he looked back at the ceiling. "Do you want me to go to my room?"

Panic rushed through her. "No," she all but shouted.

"Okay. It's okay. I won't go anywhere." He raised up on an elbow and turned toward her. "Do you want me to put clothes on?"

No, she did not want him to put clothes on. She had Jordan Grant naked in bed with her. Every coming of age fantasy she'd had was now reality.

"Emme?"

"No?"

He smiled wide. "Why did you say it like a question?"

"Well, because I basically told you I want you naked."

"Nothing wrong with that. I like you naked too."

Her entire body flamed with her blush and she pulled the covers up over her head. "This is embarrassing. Can we go back to sleep now?"

He laughed and stretched out on the bed. "Yeah. We can go back to sleep now."

CHAPTER 11

Jordan opened the door for room service to push the cart in. He didn't know how long Emme would sleep, but he was starving. After dozing for an hour, he'd woken energized and horny — along with another feeling he couldn't describe. It was almost…happy? Whatever it was, it was the exact opposite of how he'd felt for the last ten years. He'd thought about waking her, but decided to let her sleep and had gone for a run instead to try and burn off some of the excess energy.

Watching her confront her nightmares last night drove home the realization he'd made on the camping trip when he'd unfairly dumped his baggage at Bree's door. He'd never really faced his own issues. He'd pushed them down and ignored them. Kept going on deployment after deployment because that was the only place things made sense. The only place he felt needed and useful.

His conversations with Rocco and Emme came back to him. Both had found a sense of purpose in what they did. He wasn't getting that in the Army anymore — hadn't been for a while. But if he left, what else was there?

A soft sound drew his attention as he handed the receipt folder to the attendant. Emme stood inside the hall leading to her room. Thanking the young man who'd brought the food, he closed the door, and pushed the cart over to the table. "Are you hungry?"

She nodded and scratched the top of one foot with the other. Her pajama pants hung low on her hips, exposing a sliver of skin above the waistband. He'd kissed that brief expanse of skin and all the skin above and below it. His cock remembered.

Down, boy.

"I got you an omelet and fruit. I noticed that's pretty much all you eat for breakfast."

She tucked a strand of hair behind her ear. "Thanks." She walked to the table and sat.

He set her plate in front of her and grabbed the carafe from the cart. "Coffee?"

"Please."

Two words so far and she hadn't met his gaze yet. Did she have morning-after regret? Of all the thoughts he'd had while waiting for her to wake up, not touching her hadn't crossed his mind. He could feel her unease and a lead ball formed in the pit of his stomach, killing his appetite.

Her fork clattered to her plate. "I don't know how to act."

He leaned back in his chair. *Here comes the brush off.* "What do you mean?"

"What am I supposed to… Can I…?" She propped her elbow on the table and dropped her forehead into her hand. "This feels weird and I don't want it to be weird."

"How do you want it to be?" He didn't know whether to tell her they could go back to the way things were before and forget it happened or pick her up and set her in his lap.

"Not weird!"

He sighed. "Do you want to pretend it never happened?"

She finally met his gaze, a dark blush forming high on her cheek bones. "No."

"What *do* you want?"

Her tongue licked her bottom lip and she glanced at his mouth. "To touch you."

"Take what you want, Emme."

Her chair scraped on the floor and she padded around the table. He scooted his chair back and waited, his heart pounding in his chest. His cock throbbing in his pants.

She straddled him, hooked her hand behind his neck, and pressed her mouth to his.

Surprised, it took a few seconds for his brain to catch up. He wrapped his arms around her waist and pulled her closer. He pushed a hand up her shirt and pressed on her upper back, crushing her breasts to his chest. Opening his mouth he traced her lips and thrust his tongue in when she matched his movement.

She sucked on his tongue and he groaned deep in his throat. She rubbed herself against him, once. Twice. He shoved his other hand into the waistband of her pants and traced the seam of her ass. She gasped and increased the pace of her hips. He held her firm against him and thrust up to meet her.

Her panting grew heavier and her nails scraped across his scalp. She broke their kiss and dropped her head to the crook of his neck.

She shuddered in his arms and let out a low-pitched moan.

Taking his hand from under her shirt, he brushed her thick hair away from her face. "You're so fucking beautiful." She blushed and he used his thumb to tilt her chin up to look at him. "No more hiding. No more weird. Okay?"

She nodded. "Okay."

"You still hungry?"

"Yeah."

"You want to stay here or move back to your seat?"

She dropped her gaze.

"Don't be afraid to tell me what you want. There's no wrong answer."

"I want to stay here."

He couldn't stop the grin from turning up the corner of his mouth. "Yeah?"

She raised her eyes and smiled. "Yeah."

"Okay then. Stand up real quick." He helped her stand and reached across the table for her plate before pulling her back down onto his lap so both of her legs were across his.

She held her right arm close to her body and used her left to eat. He hadn't noticed she wasn't wearing her sling. "How's your arm?"

"It's a little sore."

He rubbed the top of her shoulder, keeping the pressure light. "Did we make it worse?"

She shook her head. "I don't think so."

"You need to wear your sling, babe." He didn't want her further injuring her arm.

"I don't put it on until after I've showered," she said.

The image of her, wet and soapy, invaded his mind. His fingers flexed on her hip and she squirmed in his lap.

Her eyelids drooped and she licked the corner of her mouth. "I might need some help washing my hair. My shoulder gets really tired if I hold it up for too long."

"You done eating?" he asked.

She tossed her fork on the table. "For now." Her voice was breathy, her desire palpable.

He slid his arm under her legs and stood, cradling her. "I want to check out this steam shower of yours." He strode toward her room, passed the bed, and into her spacious bathroom.

Setting her down in front of the large, walk-in shower, he hooked his thumbs into her pants. "Can I take these off?"

"Yes." Her fingers dipped into the waistband of his gym shorts. "Can I take these off?"

His dick pulsed against the fabric and she raised her eyebrows. "Is that a yes?"

He grinned. "That's a 'fuck yes'."

She pulled her fingers out of his shorts and pushed his shirt up his chest instead. "So, one for yes and two for no?"

Grabbing his shirt, he yanked it over his head. "Let's assume if he's moving, he's saying yes."

Her mouth hovered over his nipple, her warm breath making it pebble. She licked the hard nub, pulled it into her mouth, and rolled it between her teeth.

Sucking in a breath, he fisted his hands in her hair, holding her in place. "Fuck, that feels good."

Her fingers scraped down his back and into his shorts, pushing them down his legs. His hard shaft sprang free, straining toward Emme. She gripped him in her small hand and pumped him. He didn't know whether to thrust into her hand or pull away. Grabbing her wrist, he held her hand still.

"You don't like it?" she asked.

"I like it too much. You keep it up and I'm going to come all over your hand." He disengaged and opened the glass shower door, turning the faucet on until hot water and steam filled the space. "Let's get you naked."

She reached behind her neck and pulled the thin shirt over her head, keeping her bad arm by her side. He dropped to his knees and grasped the side of her panties, easing them over her hips and down her legs. His mouth lined up perfectly with her core. Using his thumbs, he opened her and pressed his tongue against her clit. Her musky scent filled his nostrils, driving his own desire higher. He wanted to spread her out on the floor and lick and suck her until she screamed his name.

"Jordan," she groaned.

He stood and backed her into the shower stall. She tilted her head back to wet her hair and he took advantage of the exposed skin of her neck. The water sluiced over his face and shoulders. He pulled back and reached for the shampoo in the recessed shelf. Pouring some into his hands, he rubbed them together to work up a lather, and ran his fingers into her hair, massaging her scalp.

She stepped closer to him, running her hands up his sides and around his back. Her head fell back and she groaned. Her eyes shone with desire.

He kissed her. Hot, open mouthed, their tongues tangling together. He tilted her head back under the stream of water and continued to work his fingers while he rinsed her hair.

This had to be one of the most erotic things he'd ever done to a woman. He could still taste her essence on his tongue, but washing her hair seemed somehow more intimate.

"Conditioner?" he asked.

Her eyes fluttered open. "What?"

Glad to see he wasn't the only one losing his senses. "Do you want conditioner in your hair?"

"If it means you keep doing what you're doing, then yes."

He smoothed conditioner through the long strands of her hair, then lathered body wash in his hands. Her heavy breasts filled his palms and he pinched her nipples between his fingers and thumbs, rolling the hard points.

Her breath hitched. "Oh god."

He traced the edge of her jaw with his tongue. "You like that?"

"Yes," she gasped.

"Does it make you wet?"

"Soaked." She clenched him in her fist and pumped her hand along his hard length. "Does this make you hard?"

Like the Rock of Gibraltar. "Fucking rigid."

Her teeth scraped his neck.

He gritted his teeth and hissed.

"Too much?"

"No. Keep going." He found her slit and traced his finger along the seam of her lips. Inch by slow inch, he inserted his middle finger into her tight core. His thumb pressed against her clit.

She rode his hand and he inserted another finger.

"I want you." Her hand pulsed around his cock. "Now."

God yes, he wanted to slide into her hot, tight heat. Feel her clench and pulse around him. "Fuck." He removed his fingers and shoved her back. "Rinse your hair. I'll be right back."

"What?"

He pushed the door open and dashed out of the shower. Hitting the tile floor, he slid, barely avoiding wiping out. He ran into the bedroom, leaving a trail of water behind him. Ripping the bedside table drawer open, he grabbed the box condoms, and ran back into the bathroom. He tore the box open, sending silver square packets flying, but managed to snatch one out of the air and slammed back into the shower.

Emme stood with her hands pressed over her mouth.

"It's not funny."

Her shoulders shook. "When you slid across the floor...." She dissolved into giggles.

"There's nothing funny about safety."

Her giggles morphed into full on laughs and she bent as the waist.

He growled, stalking the two steps it took to put him in front of her. She straightened and pulled her lips between her teeth. He crowded her against the wall and she gasped when her back hit the tile.

"You get it out of your system?" He tore the packet with his teeth and roll the condom over his hard length.

She smirked. "Why? You got something else for me?"

"Yeah, I got something else for you." He ran his hands over her hips to her ass. His fingers traced the crack of her cheeks and he teased the opening of her pussy.

Her jaw dropped and her breath escaped in a rush.

He lifted her, using his hands to spread her legs. "Wrap your legs around my waist." The head of his cock found her entrance and he pressed into her. She took him, surrounded him — and it destroyed him.

Everything in him shifted and made room for Emme. He'd buried his cock in her slick heat, but she was the one who invaded every inch of him.

He withdrew and thrust forward.

She wrapped her arms around his neck. "Oh my god." Her heels dug into his ass. "Oh god."

Scraping his teeth along her jaw, he held her in place on his cock, adjusting to the feelings coursing through him. Not just the desire or the need to slam into her and possess her. There was something spreading through his chest. Something heavy, but freeing at the same time.

He pulled out slowly until the only the tip remained and slid forward at the same pace.

Her finger nails dug into his shoulders. "Faster. Please."

"So polite. Since you asked so nicely." Jordan pressed her against the wall and surged forward. Picking up the pace, he pumped into her, keeping a quick and steady rhythm.

She nipped his earlobe. "Your cock feels so good."

His fingers dug into her ass. "What does it feel like?"

"Thick. Hard. I can feel your balls slapping my ass."

"Fuck. Hang on, babe." He lifted her higher and pistoned his hips. His balls drew up against his body and tension coiled tight at the base of his spine.

"I'm going to come. Don't stop," she panted in his ear.

"Let it go. I want to feel you milk my cock."

"Holy fuck." Her head fell back against the tile and her shout echoed off the tile walls.

Her walls clenched and pulsed around him. Watching her come — eyes closed, mouth agape, ecstasy all over her face — he shortened his strokes. The tension released and he planted himself deep in her core as his orgasm exploded. Grunting, he flexed his ass cheeks and dropped his head forward. The tile under his temple was cool — the only cool spot on his entire body. His heart pounded, threatening to break through his chest.

He tried to tell himself it was just the exertion, but Mötley Crüe's *Kickstart My Heart* started playing in his head. Why did he feel like he was in over his head?

Emme's fingers massaged the back of his neck. "You okay?" she asked.

He raised his head and kissed her softly. "You'd think I'd be in better shape, running five miles a day."

Her eyebrows rose. "Well. This is more of a sprint than a marathon."

Shifting her weight so he held her with one arm, he grasped the base of the condom and eased out of her. Her eyes closed and her lips parted in a silent gasp.

"Jesus, Emme, you're killing me."

"What?" She looked honestly confused.

He shook his head and eased her legs down, making sure she was steady before letting her go. Stepping out of the shower, he tossed the condom into the small trashcan and rejoined Emme in the shower. She stood under the water with her head tilted back, her left arm squeezing excess water from her hair—watching him with her golden eyes.

She turned off the water. "Would you hand me a towel?"

Somewhat disappointed, he grabbed a large white towel from the bar just outside the shower. She took it, bent at the waist, and wrapped it around her head. When she stood, she flipped the ends of the towel over her head. Her breasts rose and fell while she fiddled with the ends of the towel. He felt blood flowing to his cock again.

"There's a robe on the back of the door." She pointed while holding the towel on her head.

He glanced over his shoulder, then back at Emme, and raised his eyebrows.

"Jordan!"

A slow grin spread across his face. Damn, she was fun to tease.

She crossed her arms over her breasts. "It's getting cold. Get me the robe, please."

Stepping out of the stall, he pulled a towel from the bar and wrapped it around his waist before pulling the robe off the back of the door. He held it out for Emme like it was an evening coat. She turned and slid her arms into the sleeves of the robe. He pulled it over her shoulders and wrapped the sides around her, enveloping her in his arms.

He kissed her temple. "I would have preferred keeping you naked."

"Wha—?" She tilted her head to glare at him. "That was really sweet until you started talking."

He grinned and kissed her temple again.

CHAPTER 12

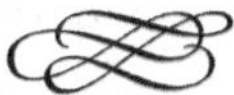

*E*mme stifled a groan and tried to keep her eyes from rolling into the back of her head as Jordan's thumbs kneaded the arch of her foot. His fingers were magic. Something he'd proven several times over the last couple of days. They'd spent a lot of time in bed. Or the floor. And the couch.

She shifted and stifled another groan for a different reason.

He stopped rubbing. "You okay?"

She looked over the top of the book she'd found, down her body and up his to where he lay with his head on the other arm rest. His green eyes stared at her with concern. "Yeah. Just getting more comfortable." He asked her that a lot — if she was okay or in pain. The foot rub was a result of her saying her feet were killing her from all the walking they did earlier that day in the souq.

At times it felt as if he were coddling her. Taking care of her because she was a responsibility instead of a desire. Then there were times like this. She didn't know too many guys who would spend an afternoon rubbing a woman's feet just because she said they hurt.

The corners of his mouth tilted and he winked before going back to watching the soccer game on TV. God, she loved his smile.

He didn't do it enough. She shouldn't complain. When he did smile, it was always directed at her.

He had moments where he seemed to get lost in his head. She knew he was worried about his unit. He checked his email at least three times a day.

They had such a finite amount of time together before they went back to their real lives. Separately. An urgency to jam as much as she could into the next week threatened to overwhelm her.

"Have you ever been married?" she asked.

He looked back at her, eyes wide. "Where did that come from?"

She shrugged and rested the book on her chest. "I was just thinking I don't know anything about what you've been doing for the last fifteen years, other than being in the Army."

"Hmm. Well, to answer your question, no. I've never been married." He pulled her other foot onto his lap and started rubbing.

"How come?"

He sighed. "Never found the right girl at the right time. I came kind of close once, but it ended up not working out."

"Why?"

His brows drew together. "You really want to know this?"

She nodded. Yes. No. Hell, she wasn't sure. She didn't even know what made her start with this line of questioning other than wanting to know more about him. Why hadn't she started with something simple like his favorite color?

"It was about six or seven years ago. We'd been dating for almost two years. I'd been deployed a couple of times and we'd made it through without any real issues. Then I got selected for Ranger school. She said she didn't want to be married to a guy that was never going to be home. She broke it off and moved out the next week."

"I'm sorry." That was such a lie. If he'd gotten married, they might not be snuggled up on the couch the way they were. No matter how fleeting the moment might be, she wouldn't have it.

He shook his head. "Don't be. I realized pretty quickly it was a good thing. I was…content when we were together. Happy even, I guess. But it didn't destroy my world when she broke it off. If I'd really loved her, it should have affected me more. What about you? Why did you get divorced?"

Her eyebrows when into her hairline. "You know I was married?"

"Got your full bio from Titan, babe."

"Ah. Right."

He shook her foot. "So. Divorced?"

It was her turn to sigh. "We dated for three years in college. It seemed like the natural progression of our relationship, but we weren't prepared for the real-world. Student loans, jobs, bills, and everything else that went with it. Being adults was nothing like being college students. We grew up and became different people."

"So no horrible, made-for-reality-TV divorce?"

"Nope. Looking back it kind of feels like we woke up one day, looked at each other, and said 'let's get divorced'."

"Do you keep in touch?"

She shook her head. "Not really. The occasional Christmas card. He's married with four kids, now."

"What's your favorite color?"

Smiling she said, "Sapphire blue. You?" He'd stolen her backup question.

"OD green."

She threw her head back and laughed. "Olive drab green is no one's favorite color."

"It is too. I remember you wore your dad's old uniform shirt to school one time. It had the Ranger tab and jump wings on it. I was so jealous."

"I remember that. I was in my grunge phase. Pretty sure I wore that thing for a month straight. Favorite movie?"

"I have to pick one?"

"Okay, favorite genre."

"Suspense. You?"

"Action."

"Really?"

"What? Did you think I was going to say rom-com?"

He shook his head and smiled. Her heart fluttered. "I don't even know what that is. Why action?"

She dropped her gaze and watched his hands on her feet. "When I was around ten, Mom left for a while. Every Friday, dad would take us to the video store to pick out a movie. Doug and I were supposed to take turns picking, but he always talked me into picking an action movie. It grew from that."

"Where'd your mom go?"

"At the time, I thought she was on a trip with my aunt. Later on, I realized she and Dad had separated for while."

Jordan's fingers stopped kneading and he squeezed her foot. "Really? I had no idea, Doug never said anything. What happened?"

"I asked her about it when I went through my divorce. Why they separated and why she stayed." She looked back at him. "Dad got orders to Fort Bragg. It was the third move in four years and she didn't know if she could do it again. It didn't help that Dad was leaving all the moving to her and doing what he always did. She said she needed to figure out if that was the life she wanted to live. If it was the life she wanted me and Doug to live. So she told Dad he needed to figure it out and she went to stay with my aunt."

"But she came back?" he asked.

"Yeah. She realized that was what she'd signed on for. It helped that Dad apologized for expecting her to take care of everything." She smiled. "I think having to deal with me and Doug by himself for a month was a big shock to his system."

"Could you do it?" His voice was low and intense.

She felt breathless. "What?"

His fingers tensed around her foot. "Live that life."

Her heart stopped. She stared into his eyes, trying to decipher his words. Was this—? Was he asking her if she wanted to live that life with him? "I grew up in that life. It was all I knew. I think that's a small reason I took the NGO job. I wanted to go some-where new. But now? Maybe—"

A knock on the door interrupted her before she could finish — *maybe for the right guy.* He tilted his head back to look. "Did you order anything from down stairs?"

"No," she said.

Moving her legs to the side of the couch, he stood, and kissed her before walking to the door and looking through the peephole. He opened the door a crack. "Yes?"

"Jordan Grant?" a woman's voice asked.

Emme sat up on the couch so she could see over the back.

"Yes."

"Is Emmeline France here as well?"

"Who are you?" he demanded.

"I should have introduced myself first. I'm Alicia Broadmore from the American Embassy. I have your and Ms. France's passports."

Jordan opened the door farther and the woman entered the suite. She stopped just inside the door and waited for Jordan to close it.

Emme stood and walked around the end of the couch. Dressed in a tan suit and low brown heels, she presented the epitome of professional woman.

"Ms. France?" she asked.

"Yes."

Alicia stepped forward, with her hand outstretched. "It's a pleasure to meet you. I'm glad to see you are, in fact, safe. We've seen the news that you were rescued, of course, but with no one having heard from you in person, there's been speculation that the reports were false."

Emme shook her hand. "No, they're true."

"I figured that when I was told the passport request came through Titan."

Jordan stood by Emme and rested his hand on her lower back. "You know Titan?"

Alicia's eyes flickered to Jordan's hand. "Only by reputation." She reached into her bag and pulled out two passports and a pen. "If you'll sign the passports, I'll be out of your hair."

She flipped open one of the passports before handing it to Jordan and handed the other one to Emme without opening it.

"What about visa's?" Emme asked, taking the passport.

"They've already been stamped, showing you entered a week ago," Alicia said.

Emme raised her eyebrows and looked at Alicia, her question evident.

Alicia smiled. "Titan has a lot of connections in Abu Dhabi."

"No kidding," Emme said. Getting back-dated visa stamps was no little accomplishment. Even after everything, she didn't know whether to be impressed or scared. Maybe impressively scared.

She and Jordan signed the passports and handed the pen back to Alicia. Taking it she said, "Mr. Westin asked that you call him before you make flight arrangements to return to the U.S." She handed Emme a business card. "Feel free to call if you need anything in the interim."

She took the offered card. "Thank you."

Alicia hesitated a moment, then stepped forward and hugged Emme. "I'm very glad to know you're safe."

At a loss for words, Emme stood there while Alicia released her. "Uh. Thank you?"

"Sorry. I probably should have asked first." She rubbed Emme's arm awkwardly. "Well, I'll leave you alone. Enjoy the rest of your stay in Abu Dhabi."

She let herself out of the suite and Jordan made sure the door was closed.

Emme stared down at her new passport. "Do we have to stay here?"

"What do you mean?"

Her stomach fluttered, unsure whether she should ask the next question. "Can we leave Abu Dhabi?"

He shoved his hands into his pants pockets and hunched his shoulders. "You mean go back to the States?"

"No, not yet." She looked at her passport briefly. "Can we go somewhere else? There's not a lot to do here other than the souq and the Grand Mosque and we've already done that."

"Where were you thinking?"

"Rome?" She shrugged. "I've never been and I've always wanted to see Saint Peter's and the Vatican."

"Let me clear it with Jared, but I don't think he'll have an issue with it." He smiled. "Roman holiday, huh?"

She grinned. "Yeah."

~

"Give me two days, we've got something in the works," Jared said.

Jordan looked over to where Emme sat on the corner of the couch, watching him over the back. "Sounds good."

"Parker'll email you the itinerary later today. It'll take you back to the U.S., with a stop over in Rome."

"Thanks, man."

"No problem." His voice became muffled as he said something to someone off the line. "Watch the news tonight." The phone disconnected.

Jordan tossed the phone on the table next to the couch and sat close to Emme.

"What did he say?"

"He said give him a couple of days to make the reservations. Parker'll send us the reservation information."

Joy lit up her face. All the air left his lungs like she'd sucker punched him and he swore his heart stopped. Her resiliency amazed him. The smallest things made her happy. When was the last time he'd found pleasure in the small things?

"What?" Her eyebrows pinched together.

"Come here." He pulled her onto his lap so she straddled him.

Her hands went to his shoulders. "We need to make hotel reservations."

"I've got a buddy that was stationed in northern Italy — I'll shoot him an email and see if he has any recommendations." He found the hem of her shirt and pushed his hands underneath, running his palms up the smooth skin of her back.

"Fatima's going to be here soon."

That wasn't why he pulled her onto his lap — he just wanted her close — but now she'd put the idea in his head. "Are you saying you don't have time to have your way with me?"

"Whatever." She rolled her eyes and he laughed.

Her skin was smooth against his palms. He was an addict getting his fix. Only his drug was Emme. Her skin. Her smile. He wanted to wrap her in his arms. Protect her, keep her safe and happy, and never let her go.

That reality didn't exist. In a week he had to let her go and watch her walk away.

What if he didn't, though? What if there was a way to keep this thing between them going? See where it took them.

The electronic whir of the door lock stopped him from voicing the ideas playing havoc in his mind. Emme scrambled off his lap and tucked a strand of hair behind her ear.

Fatima entered the suite, calling out a greeting, and Emme shot up from the couch like someone had lit a fire under her gorgeous butt. He smirked, not giving one fuck about anyone seeing them together.

Scooting forward, he flipped the laptop open, and logged onto his Army webmail. An email from Parker topped the list of his inbox. Clicking on the attachment, he opened their itinerary. They'd been booked on an early morning flight the day after tomorrow. The body of Parker's email simply said: *Here you go. Watch the 1800 BBC news broadcast.*

He looked at his watch. Emme could decide whether they'd order in or go out after the news.

The next email was from his sergeant with a watered down update. All the secret and operational information had been stripped out, but he could read between the lines. They were busy and going out almost every night. His sergeant thought the new lieutenant was an asshat and wanted to know when Jordan would be getting there.

He dropped his head in his hands. For the first time in his career, he hated his job. Not just questioned his purpose and mission, but hated that the Army was pulling him away from something he wanted. Maybe that was the problem. Everything he'd ever wanted had been provided by the Army. He'd never wanted something as much as he wanted Emme.

But he had a mission. Orders to follow. An oath to uphold and men and women counting on him. He couldn't ignore all that. Not even for her.

The bedroom door opened and he closed the laptop without responding to the email. He'd take care of it later.

The ladies stopped next to the couch and he stood.

"It was a pleasure meeting you, Major Grant." Fatima laid her hand over her heart and bowed her head briefly. "Dr. Tuska informed me you and Ms. France are departing soon."

"Yes. The day after tomorrow."

"Then I wish you both a safe journey home."

"Thank you," he said.

Emme walked Fatima to the door where they hugged. She came back to the couch after closing the door behind Fatima. "Is everything alright?"

He sat and pulled her down next to him. "Yeah. Why?"

"You looked stressed when we came out of the room."

"Got an email from my sergeant. The new L.T. Is making his life hell."

"Isn't that what lieutenants are supposed to do?"

He smirked. "Yeah."

Her eyes searched his face. "Anything else?"

He shook his head. No need to unload on her. She was dealing with her own issues. "Parker said to watch the news on BBC at six tonight. You want to order room service or go out after?"

"We can eat downstairs. Any idea why he wants us to watch?"

He shook his head. "Nope. Jared said he had something in the works and to watch the news." He pulled her across his lap so she straddled him again. "What were we doing before we were interrupted?"

"Um." She pursed her lips and lowered her gaze.

"What?"

She averted her gaze.

He wiggled her hips. "Emme. What?"

"I'm a little sore," she whispered.

He pulled his lips between his teeth, forcing down the urge to bang on his chest and roar. It might make him a Neanderthal, but he was oddly satisfied that he'd fucked her so well she was sore. He trailed the back of his fingers across the side of her neck and watched goose bumps form on her skin. "How about if we make out like horny teenagers?"

Sliding her hands up his chest and around his neck, she leaned forward. "Hmm. Well, I was definitely a horny teenager," she said against his lips.

"Yeah?" The skin under the hem of her shirt was warm and smooth. His entire hand could span her back.

She trailed her lips across his cheek. "I had the worst crush on you in middle school."

Shivers shot down his spine when she pulled his earlobe between her teeth. "Just middle school?" His voice sounded low, even to him. He palmed her breasts, rubbing her hard nipples through the material of her bra.

A groan rumbled deep in her throat and her breath fanned across his cheek. Soft hands skimmed under his shirt. "Maybe high school too, but you weren't around as much then."

Because he'd spent most summers avoiding her.

The tips of her fingers traced up his abs to his chest, leaving her own trail of goose bumps in their wake. "All the girls at school were jealous that my older brother was your best friend. They all tried to find out when you'd be at my house so they could invite themselves over."

He nipped the edge of her jaw. "I always wondered why there were so many girls at your house."

"They wanted to be where I am right now." She rolled her hips.

He dropped one hand to her lower back and pulled her closer, thrusting up. Threading the fingers of his other hand into her hair at the base of her neck, he pulled her mouth to his.

She opened for him, her lips soft and pliant. Her tongue met his and they dueled for control. Parry. Thrust. Taking and giving in equal measure.

Her fingernails flicked his nipples and he groaned, pulling her down hard on his lap. She answered with her own groan and rocked against his rock hard shaft.

He drew back from her mouth and sucked in a breath. "We should go for a walk."

Emme blinked a few times like she'd just woken. "Huh? Why?"

"Because I want to bury my cock balls deep in you and you can't right now," he explained, thrusting his hips up again.

"Oh."

That word almost did him in, spoken somewhere between a gasp and a sigh.

She licked her lips,. "We could—"

"No. I'd rather delay gratification and wait for later."

Rounding her back, she dropped her forehead to his shoulder. "Shit. Sorry."

He shrugged his shoulder, forcing her head up. Cradling her chin in his hand, he ran his thumb over her bottom lip, swollen from kissing. "Babe, quit apologizing. Being sexy as fuck is not something to be sorry about."

"I—" She looked shocked. Like no one had ever told her she was beautiful. Given the chance, he'd tell her every day.

He dropped a soft kiss on the tip of her nose. "It's almost six anyway. Why don't we order room service and we can continue this over dessert."

A perfectly arched eyebrow rose. "Dessert?"

"Yeah. I think we're going to need to put down a towel." He smirked. "I have a huge sweet tooth."

∼

*E*mme stared wide-eyed at the television, the stuffed grape leaf half way to her mouth. "Oh my god."

"What?" Jordan asked. He looked at the TV. A man was being put into a police car, his hands cuffed behind his back.

Dropping her food on a plate, she grabbed the remote from the floor. "Does this have—?" She pressed a button and jerked the remote as if moving it would make the TV do what she wanted it to. She rewound to the beginning of the segment.

The British reporter's voice filled the suite. *"Doctor Bennedict Wormwell, a physician with Medical Relief United, was arrested by Interpol today at his London offices on charges of human trafficking and aiding terror groups. It is believed Doctor Wormwell fed information to militia groups in African and Middle East countries where they would kidnap international aid works for ransom. He was most recently connected to the kidnapping of American Emmeline France from a non-profit clinic in Mali. A spokesman for the France family has confirmed Ms. France was rescued several days ago. He further stated she is safe in an undisclosed location while she recuperates from her ordeal. In local news—"*

She muted the TV and looked at him. "Is that what Jared was talking about?"

"Unless he knew you'd be worried about the status of the pound," he said, trying to gauge her reaction.

"Smart ass." Glaring, she picked up her food. "Remind me never to piss off Titan."

"That's probably a good life goal to have." He wiped his fingers and dropped the napkin on his plate. "You good other wise? About…" he pointed to the television.

She tilted her head and chewed. "I don't know. Part of me is glad he was arrested, but a part of me is upset he didn't get the ever-loving crap beat out of him in the process."

He threw his head back against the couch and laughed. "Are you always this blood thirsty?"

She shrugged. "Not always. Just when people get me kidnapped and almost killed."

Sobering, he lost his smile. "You're right. He needed the crap beat out of him." He tilted his head at the remnants of the picnic spread out on the floor in the front of them. "You done?"

Contemplating their dinner, she snagged the last grape leaf and popped it in her mouth. "Yeah."

"Good." He gathered the plates from the towel spread on the floor and put them on the table under the television console. Grabbing the remote from the floor, he turned off the TV and threw the remote on the couch. "Time for dessert."

CHAPTER 13

*E*mme worked her jaw, trying to relieve the pressure build up in her ears as she gazed across the small pond at the cream marble Temple of Asclepius, named for the Greek god of medicine — she'd Googled it the day they found it while walking through the Borghese gardens. They'd toured all over the city and this park, at the top of the Spanish Steps, was her favorite spot. Even with the tourists and locals walking around the crushed stone paths, and school children shrieking in the background, she could pretend it was only the two of them ensconced in their own private paradise.

Not for the first time, she wondered how she got there. A month ago, she'd been sweating her ass off in Africa. Now she was dozing in the late summer sun in Rome.

With Jordan Grant. Her school girl crush and the man she'd tried hard not to fall in love with. Tried and failed. No matter how much her mind said it was the intense circumstances of their situation, her heart wouldn't listen.

In two short days this fantasy would be over. She'd be back home and he'd be deployed back to Africa.

She had so much to say. So many questions bombarding her

mind, but the possible answers scared the crap out of her. What if he didn't want the same things she did?

W2D2? Grab the proverbial bull by the horns. The answer's always 'no' if you don't ask.

"You awake?" She tilted her head back where it rested in the pocket of his shoulder.

The hand on her hip squeezed and he grunted. She smiled, having learned over the last week that he was slow to wake. "Jordan?"

"I'm awake." His voice was low and rumbled deep in his chest under her ear.

Her heart stuttered and she took a bracing breath. "What happens next?" she asked softly.

"You mentioned the Trevi Fountain at night. We can wander over that way." He kept his eyes closed, his head resting on the arm bent under his head.

"No. I mean what happens when we leave Rome? When you— When I—" Crap. How did she ask this without actually asking?

He rolled suddenly and loomed over her, his hips pressing into hers. Caging her in with his arms braced on either side of her.

His green eyes were intense and his pupils jumped back and forth as he searched her face. "What happens between us when we get back to the real world?"

Her breathing was shallow and her fight-or-flight instinct kicked in — torn between wanting to forget she even asked and hoping he wanted the same thing. "Yeah. Do we shake hands and chalk it up to an intense experience, or—?"

"We definitely do not shake hands." His voice was adamant and as intense as his gaze.

"Oh." She traced the edge of his jaw. "Then what—?"

"What do you want, Emme?"

She licked her lips. "I don't want this to be over when we get back to the States and you deploy."

"Then we'll figure it out. People do it all the time. I'm only going to be deployed for four or five months by the time I get on the ground. We'll Skype and when I get back we'll figure things out." He brushed a strand of hair away from her temple. "Are you going to go back and work for the NGO?"

She shook her head. "No. I'm not going to put my family through that again. Mom said she and Dad would support whatever I decided, but she had that tone in her voice that said she really meant 'absolutely not'."

His body visibly relaxed. "Good."

"Besides, I'm not brave enough to slap Titan in the face by going back after they rescued me. I'm pretty sure I'd get a phone call over that one."

He smirked and pressed a quick kiss to her lips. "Good call."

"So…" She swallowed hard, trying to force her pounding heart back down into her chest. "I should focus my job search in the south east?"

"Yes, Emme. You should definitely focus your job search in the south east. Specifically in North Carolina. I hear there's some really good hospitals in Raleigh."

Relief exploded in her chest and she grinned. "Okay."

His perfect smile answered hers, right before he dropped his head. Firm lips took hers, the short blonde scruff he'd let grow scratching the skin around her lips. She didn't care. He'd left beard burn over her entire body. She loved his mouth on her.

His tongue pressed against her lips and she opened, gasping as he took control.

One hand dove under his shirt and up the wide expanse of his back as the other wound around his neck, locking him in place.

High-pitched giggling broke the spell. They pulled apart and tilted their heads back. Three young girls stood at the edge of the path watching them.

Jordan looked at her, amusement sparkling in his eyes. "Come on, before they whip out their phones and start taking pictures."

~

They wandered away from the Trevi Fountain, meandering through cobblestoned side streets. It was their last night in Rome and Jordan was determined to hit all the highlights and places Emme had said were her favorite. He pulled her hand around his back and dropped his arm over her shoulders, tucking her into his side.

She tilted her head back to look at him and he kissed her as they walked. His reward was a smile and a sparkle in her eyes. He committed that look to memory so he could pull it up when he rejoined his unit next week.

"Dinner in Piazza Navona?" he asked.

"Are you sure? We've eaten there three times already."

"The food's good and their house wine is the best we've found."

"Good point."

He kissed her temple and pulled her around a family taking pictures.

"Do you think they'll give it to us to go?"

"We can ask. Why?"

Her hand dropped down and squeezed his ass. "It's our last night here. I'd rather spend it in the apartment."

Stopping, he pulled her into his arms. "We can always get some penne all'arrabbiata and a bottle of wine on the way."

She smiled and licked her lips. "I like that idea a lot better."

He cradled the back of her head and drew her in for a kiss. Her mouth was soft and welcoming. He cursed the distance back to their apartment. Releasing her, he grabbed her hand and picked up his pace to the main road a few yards ahead of them. No more meandering.

They reached the road and he scanned for the closest taxi stand, leading Emme to the car at the head of the line.

The white cab pulled to the curb in front of them and he opened the back door, ushering Emme into the car. "*Via Ceriani*

Antonio, per favore." He slammed the door and the taxi jerked into traffic. Emme slid into him as the taxi driver took an especially sharp turn, weaving around a parked car.

What might have taken thirty minutes in normal circumstances, took half that time. When in Rome. He passed the driver the fare and exited, reaching in to help Emme climb out. She pressed a hand over her stomach and took a deep breath.

"You okay?" he asked.

"I'm glad we walked most of the time. I don't think my stomach would have taken that every day."

The corners of his mouth quirked up. "Sorry, I didn't want to wait to get you back here."

"Oh, I'm okay with that."

Her voice was breathless again. Christ, that sound could bring him to his knees. He took her hand. "Come on. Let's get pasta and wine."

Twenty minutes later, they climbed the stairs to the third floor apartment. They'd lucked out finding an apartment so close to Saint Peter's — they could actually see the dome from the roof. "Roof or apartment?" he asked. He could at least try to throw some ambiance at noodles and house wine.

She looked over her shoulder at him. "Apartment?" She stopped on the landing of their floor.

He stood on the step below, putting them eye-to-eye. "Why are you saying that like a question?"

"Because if we go to the roof we have to clean up and take everything back downstairs, but if we stay here, we can just leave everything on the counter and clean it up later."

His booming laugh filled the close stairwell. "So you're saying you want to eat and have your way with me."

Her smile was sultry. "Well, if having my way with you involves getting your tongue on my clit, then yes."

His cock couldn't be any harder than if she'd dropped to her knees and unzipped his pants. He stepped up on the landing, crowding her back. "Get in the apartment Emme and take your clothes off."

Her pupils dilated. Chest rising and falling, she spun and dug in her pocket for the apartment key. He followed as she rushed through the door, setting the pizza and bag with the wine on the table in front of the couch.

She'd kicked her shoes off in the living room and dropped her shirt a few steps from it in the short hall leading to the bedroom. Following the trail of clothes, he tore his shirt off and tossed it on the floor. For every article of Emme's clothing he found, he took off his own and left it next to hers.

She stood in the center of the small bedroom, clad only in her polka dot underwear. "Panties, Emme."

Her nipples hardened as he watched. "I thought I'd leave those for you."

His dick pulsed and he felt a drop of moisture escape. "On the bed."

She walked backward until she hit the bed, then sat and scooted back, watching him the whole time. Bracing a hand on the end of the bed, he crawled to her. He stopped halfway up her body and hooked his fingers into the edge of her underwear, drawing it down over her hips. She bent her knees and pulled her feet free.

Running his hands from her ankles up to her knees, he pressed her legs apart. "Open for me, Emme."

Her back arched slightly, pushing her hips up, and her legs fell open. Out of the corner of his eye he saw her fists clench in the bed covers. Her breasts rose and fell with each shallow breath.

He'd barely touched her. Not the way he wanted to. Not the way he was going to.

He planned on worshiping her body all night. Showing her exactly how much she meant to him.

Showing her he loved her.

It was too soon to say the words, but he knew she was it for him.

Trailing his tongue along the inside of her thigh, he moved higher, wedging his shoulders between her legs. He nipped the soft fleshy skin at the top of her thigh. She hissed in a breath and one of her hands grasped at his hair, still too short for her to do anything other than thread her fingers through.

Using his thumbs, he spread her apart. She was wet and ready for him. Her hips rolled in small circles, seeking relief. He touched her clit with the tip of his tongue.

"Uhn." Her body bowed off the bed like he had shocked her.

Fuck she was responsive.

He pressed her clit more firmly and pushed his thumb into her, twisting it.

"God, yes."

He grinned and circled his tongue around her sensitive nub. He wasn't god, but he definitely planned on showing her heaven.

Her hips moved faster, setting a regular rhythm. "More," she breathed. "Please."

Ask and you shall receive. He didn't stop moving his tongue. Pulling out his thumb, he replaced it with his first two digits, rotating and curling them to rub the front wall of her sweet pussy.

She gasped. He hooked his other hand around her hip to hold her still and close to his mouth, not letting her move away to find relief. The muscles of her channel rippled around his fingers, indicating she was close.

He didn't know if he wanted her to come on his face or around his cock. Maybe he could do both. Rising to his knees with his fingers still buried deep, he grabbed a condom from a pile on the table beside the bed.

Her eyes flew open. "Oh! No!"

"Hang on, babe." He tore the condom open with his teeth and pulled the rubber circle out, spitting the packet to the floor. He leaned down and circled her clit again with his tongue.

She held him in place with her hands on the back of his head. He took his fingers out and replaced them with his tongue, while he rolled the condom on. He thrust into her tight opening, then circled her clit. He went back and forth, never staying in one spot long enough for her orgasm to build.

Her growl of frustration, accompanied by her knees clenching the sides of his head, told him she was close but couldn't reach the finish line. Not without him.

Shoving his hands under her ass, he lifted her hips and shoved his tongue into her again.

Her nails bit into his scalp and she moaned. "Yes. There. Oh, fuck. Yes."

Her inner muscles began to ripple. He released her hips, pressed his thumb against the hood of her clit, and thrust his engorged cock into her slick, hot sheath.

"Jordan!" Her legs locked around his hips and she threw her head back as she came.

He withdrew and pushed forward again. His balls drew up and he tried to hold off. He wanted her orgasm to last, to draw out until she begged for mercy, but he didn't think he was going to last that long.

She clenched and unclenched around him, trying to milk his cock as he thrust into her. In his mind, he started to break down his M-4 rifle, listing the parts and their functions. Anything to stave off blowing his load too soon.

A shudder wracked her body and he gritted his teeth. He watched her come down from her high, her breasts rosy and flushed, a matching hue high on her cheeks. He continued to thrust into her as her muscles relaxed one by one. Her eyes fluttered and he buried himself all the way in, balls flush with her ass.

"You didn't come."

"Not yet. I want you to come again."

"I don't think that's going to happen."

He sat back on his knees, pulled her legs from around his

waist, and propped her calves on his shoulders. "I think we can make it happen."

She shook her head. "I've never had more than one orgasm while having sex, Jordan."

He withdrew slowly, until only the tip of his cock was in her. "Challenge accepted." He thrust forward and she sucked in a breath. He rubbed small, hard circles around the hood of her clit while he stayed buried inside her.

"You've had more than one orgasm while someone's played with your clit, right?"

Her breath escaped in a gasp. "Yes."

"So if I play with your clit while my cock's buried in your tight, wet pussy you'll probably come again, right?"

"Maybe." Her hips jerked.

Yeah, she was going to come again. He continued to rub his thumb in circles, first one direction, then the other. A flush started to spread across her chest again. He let go of her calf where he held it and pinched her nipple.

"Oh, fuck." Her teeth bit her bottom lip and her head fell to the side.

He pulled out and slammed forward. "That's right, Emme. Feel it. Can you feel my cock pulsing in you?"

"Yes," she gasped. Her breathing was nothing but gasps. He switched hands, pinching her other nipple and rubbing her clit in the other direction.

"Shit. Jordan, please."

He withdrew and thrust again. "Please what?" He wanted to possess her. Destroy her for all other men, because there was never going to be anyone else for her.

"Fuck, make me come. Move. Do something!"

He twisted her nipple, slammed forward, and pulled on her clit at the same time.

She screamed and her walls clamped down on his cock. That was what he needed. He fell forward and braced his weight on his hands, driving his dick into her pussy as she came again. It took only seconds for his orgasm to explode out of him.

He threw his head back and roared. Her legs fell to his waist and he buried himself to the hilt. Collapsing forward, he kept enough sense to brace his weight. Her hand found the side of his face and he pressed a kiss to her palm before kissing her mouth.

"Told you you could do it."

A satisfied smile played at her mouth. "I don't think I survived it though."

Jordan rolled to the side and kissed the space between her breasts. "We'll find out after we eat."

"Huh?"

He winked and got up to throw away the condom and get the food. She was going to need her strength for round two.

She eyed her parents' modest, two-story colonial house nestled in an older suburb of Newport News, as Jordan turned into the drive-way, trying to shift through the feelings raging through her.

Jordan eased to a stop, shoved it in to park, and shut off the engine. He leaned close and rubbed his nose behind her ear. "You okay?"

Turning her head, she gave him a tight smile. "I'm nervous ." And scared, but she didn't admit that to him.

"About what?" His voice was soft and deep, smoothing over the edges of her emotions.

She took a deep breath. How to articulate everything she was feeling? "Mom's going to cry. And then I'm going to cry."

"Okay." His brow narrowed in that way guys do when they have no idea what a woman is saying.

"And as soon as we walk in that house, we're over."

Jordan reared back from her. "What?"

She winced at his shout in the tight confines of the car. "Not like that," she rushed on. "But when we get out of this car, it's not just us anymore. The bubble we've been in is going to pop." She dropped her gaze to her clenched fingers. "I want to stay in the bubble."

God, she sounded desperate. And needy. She hated being that clingy, needy girl who couldn't stand on her own two feet, but all he'd done for the last two weeks was take care of her. She wanted him to know she needed *him*, not what he could do for her.

"Emme." He threaded his fingers into her hair and she nuzzled his hand cupping the side of her face. "Babe, look at me."

The backs of her eyes stung when she lifted her gaze.

"Is that why you didn't want them to meet us at the airport?" The pad of his thumb brushed back and forth on her cheek.

"Partly. Mostly I didn't want a huge scene in the middle of baggage claim."

He dropped his forehead to hers. "It'll be okay. Our bubble won't pop. We'll have to make it a little bigger." He kissed her forehead, then the corner of her eye. "You ready to go in?"

Taking a bracing breath, she nodded.

"Come on. The sooner your mom starts crying, the sooner she'll stop."

Emme smiled and released her seat belt. Opening the door, the pressure in her ears finally equalized.

Pop.

~

He pulled their suitcases out of the trunk of the rental car and slammed the lid closed. Throwing the straps of his black duffle bag over his shoulder, he took Emme's hand and grabbed the handle of her larger, rolling suitcase.

He wasn't sure if she believed his reassurances. He needed her to because he needed to believe them too. She was right in some regards — everything would be different from this point forward. There was no escaping that, but they would make it work.

The front door opened and an older version of Emme ran out

and down the steps, catapulting herself at Emme. She was crying. Her shoulders shook with the force of her sobs and Emme had her head buried in her mom's neck.

Her dad came down the steps more slowly, but that may have been to give himself a few seconds to gather his composure.

Jordan held out his hand. "General."

The older man pulled him into a bear hug and pounded his back. "Thanks for bringing my girl home." His voice caught at the end and he cleared his throat. He released Jordan and clapped him on the shoulder.

"Quit fussing Lori and let me in." General France grasped his wife's shoulders and pulled her back a step and to the side. He took her place and wrapped Emme in his arms, picking her up off the ground.

"Hi, Daddy," Emme whispered.

"Never again, Emmeline."

"Yes, Daddy."

"Okay." He set her down and held her by the shoulders. "Well." He cleared his throat again. "Let's go inside and quit giving the neighbors a show." He took the handle of her suitcase and led the way up the steps and over the threshold.

Her mom went ahead of her, giving Jordan the chance to trail his fingers across her lower back. He bit back a grin when she shivered.

"Behave," she hissed over her shoulder.

Letting his hand trail down, he patted her on the ass.

She whipped around and glared at him. If she thought he was going to spend the next day and a half not touching her, she'd left her good sense back in Rome. Winking, he gave her a small push to get her moving.

"I'll get you two settled in your rooms." Emme's mom led the way up the stairs leading off the small foyer.

He took Emme's suitcase from her father and trailed after them.

"Do you need a nap? Or a shower? Doug and Gilly are coming for dinner. I told them around five. I'm making chicken and dumplings. I know I usually only make it when it's cold outside, but it's your favorite."

She turned left at the top of the stairs. "Jordan, I have you down at this end." She pointed to the door on the right at the end of the hall. "Emme, you're in the room next to me and Dad."

Screw that B.S. Emme wasn't going to sleep anywhere other than next to him.

"Mom." Emme took her hands. "Calm down. We're fine. A nap will be good and dinner sounds wonderful."

Her mom sniffled and nodded, then pulled Emme into her arms again. Jordan went into his assigned bedroom and closed the door to give them some privacy. Mrs. France had been talking a mile a minute on the climb up the stairs. Probably a mix of nervousness and excitement with a whole lot of relief thrown in for good measure. Not that he could blame her — it wasn't every day your daughter was snatched from the clutches of death and whisked off to a secret location.

Dropping his bag at the foot of the full bed, he flopped down in the center. The whole thing was surreal. He didn't know if he felt more like Alice lost in Wonderland or the caterpillar trying to figure out who the hell the weird chick was.

Someone tapped twice on his door and he sat up. "Come in."

Emme squeezed through the door and closed it softly behind her. She walked directly to him, straddled his lap, wrapped her arms around him, and buried her face in his neck.

He draped his arms around her waist. "You wanna talk about it?"

"My mom is very emotional." Her voice was muffled against his skin.

"Stands to reason."

"I know. I needed someone calm."

The ache in his chest warred with the pride he felt in her trust.

Was that all she needed him for? A guarantee that he'd have her back, no matter what, no matter who. She'd as much implied their time together was almost over. She'd said that wasn't what she'd meant, but the sadness in her eyes had made him question her assurances.

Time would tell. Time with him gone and her settling back into her life. But right now, he wanted to keep pretending it was still the two of them in their bubble. "You wanna take a nap in here?"

She nodded against his neck.

Grasping the back of her neck, he pulled her head up and brushed her thick hair away from her face. "Stand up, babe." She stood and he scooted back in the bed. Crawling up next to him, she burrowed into him again, tucking her head under his chin, and throwing her leg over his hips.

He cocooned her in his arms. "That's going to have to wait 'till tonight. I'm not going down to dinner smelling like sex."

She tried to punch him in side, but didn't have the leverage to pull back enough. "Ass."

Smiling against her temple, he said, "I'm not kidding. You're going to have to sneak in here after your parents go to sleep."

"I was already planning on it."

"You dirty girl," he teased.

"Go to sleep, perv."

He rubbed his chin against the top of her head, smiling. He'd show her perv later.

~

His eyes snapped open with the soft slide of the door as it opened. Raising his head, he caught Mrs. France backing out of the door, a small smiled on her face.

Busted.

Oh, well. Her parents would find out he and Emme were

together eventually. She snored softly in his arms. He ran his hand up and down her back. "Emme. Time to wake up."

"Mmm." She rubbed her face in his neck and moved closer.

He traced her cheek with his thumb. "Rise and shine, sleeping beauty."

She put her hand over his and moved it down to her chest, manipulating his hand to plump and rub her breast.

Blood shot straight to his cock. Fuck. They didn't have time.

"Babe, your mom came in to check on us. We should probably get up."

In one motion, her eyes flew open and she rolled away from him, off the bed. She stood with her hands braced on the edge of the mattress. "What?"

Propping himself up on an elbow, he grinned. "She poked her head in and checked on us."

She pushed her hair away from her face. "What did you do? Did she say anything?"

He chuckled. "She didn't say anything. I woke you up."

"Oh my god. My mom caught me in bed with a guy." She covered her face with her hands. "This is so embarrassing."

"Why? You were married. I'm pretty sure she knows you're not a virgin. Besides, we're fully clothed."

She dropped her hands to her hips. "Jordan!"

"What? I don't think she was upset." He sat up and swung his legs off the bed. "She didn't barge in and demand I quit defiling her only daughter." Walking around the bed, he pulled her into a loose hug.

"Fine, but don't blame me if my dad shoots you when we get downstairs."

Laughing, he kissed the side of her neck. "I think we'll be good. I'm going to hit the head first."

"Okay."

She moved to pull away. "Not yet. I haven't tasted you in hours." Cupping the back of her head, he took her mouth. She opened under him with a small moan, her tongue surging forward to tangle with his. She raised up on her toes, wrapping her arms around his neck and pressing her body closer.

The weight of her breasts pushed against his chest and his erection strained against the zipper of his pants. Groaning, he ended the kiss, resting his forehead against hers. "I definitely need a few extra minutes before I go downstairs."

"Please don't walk downstairs with a hard-on."

"I'll take care of it."

Her head jerked up. "Oh my god! Don't do that either!"

He threw his head back and laughed. "There are other ways to get rid of a hard-on besides jacking off."

"Huh."

"What's huh?"

"I've never thought about it before. Girls don't have to worry about those things."

"Yeah, guess not." He swatted her on the butt. "Come on. Let's go face the firing squad."

"Keep joking. It's all fun and games until I have to dig a bullet out of your ass."

He shook his head and wrapped an arm around her shoulder, leading her to the door. "Go on. I'll be down in a minute." Giving her a small push toward the stairs, he entered the hall bath and closed the door. Several minutes later, he bound down the stairs and followed the sound of voices to the kitchen.

Doug pushed away from the counter with a hand outstretched. "Jordan. Welcome back." Jordan wasn't surprised when Doug pulled him into a bro hug and pounded on his back. "Thanks. I—" He stepped back. "Thanks."

Jordan slapped him on the shoulder and scanned the room for Emme. She stood with her father in the adjoining breakfast nook. Her head rested against his chest with her arms wrapped around his waist. They'd always been close. An image of a little girl with Emme's curls running to him flashed in his mind.

That's what he wanted. The piece of him he never realized was missing.

"You want a beer?" Doug asked.

He tore his gaze away from father and daughter. "Yeah."

"They're in the garage."

He turned, but Jordan stopped him. "I'll grab it. Where's the garage?"

Doug pointed to the door on the other side of Emme and her father. "Through that door. Fridge's is on the left."

He edged around Emme as her dad moved back. "I'm grabbing a beer. Do either of you want one?"

Emme shook her head. "I'll come with you," General France said. He followed Jordan through the door into the two-car garage.

Jordan opened the fridge and pulled two Sam Adams lagers from the door. He held one out. "General."

Taking the proffered beer he leaned against the work bench. "You're sleeping with my daughter. I think you can call me Emmard."

Jordan froze. Even though he detected no censure, he didn't know how to take the general's words. "Sir, I want you to know that I care for Emme."

"Jordan, you can be very sure if I didn't believe that, you wouldn't be here right now." He twisted off the bottle top and threw it in the trash next to the fridge. "I read Titan's after action report. I know you volunteered to stay with her, even though they had someone else lined up." He took a swig of his beer. "I also know how close she came to being killed."

"She's safe, Sir."

He took another pull of his beer and nodded. "When do you join back up with your unit?"

"I leave here in the morning. There's a flight leaving out of Fort Bragg in two days."

"Thank you, for going to get her. I know it probably seems

ridiculous…you weren't really needed, to be honest. But it was a comfort to Lori knowing someone who knew Emme would be there when she was rescued." He looked at Jordan and gave him a level stare. "Someone she would be comfortable with after everything we imagined happened to her."

"I understand, sir."

He pushed away from the bench. "Come one. Let's go back in before Lori comes looking for us."

Jordan followed Emmard back into the house. Emme caught his eye and raised her eyebrows, silently asking if everything was okay. He nodded his head and sent her a quick smile. Relief softened her face. Had she really been afraid her dad would shoot him? He took a drink of his beer to hide his smile.

CHAPTER 15

"That's not how it happened." Doug walked into the dining room after clearing the last of the dishes away.

"Yes, it is!" Emme followed with a glass of wine for her mom. "That's exactly how it happened and I was the one that got grounded for two weeks."

"No, it's not."

"Mom!"

"Don't drag me into this, sweetie. This is between you and your brother." Her mom shook her head and sipped her wine.

Jordan dropped his arm over the back of her chair. "Admit it, Emme Lou Who, you were the one who broke the window."

Emme gasped. "Don't you start, Jingle Balls! You were just as much to blame!" She tried to scoot her chair away from him while sitting, annoyed that he and her brother were still trying to pin the broken front window on her after all these years, but he grabbed the bottom and wouldn't let her move.

"What's with the nicknames?" Gilly asked.

Doug kissed her temple. "Emme's full name is Emmeline Louise. I don't remember when we started calling her Emme Lou, but it morphed at some point to Emme Lou Who. I think one year around Christmas after we watched *How the Grinch Stole Christmas*?" He looked at Emme for confirmation.

She stuck her tongue out at him, causing Gilly to grin.

"What about Jingle Balls?" Gilly asked. "Is that from the same thing?"

"I don't remember," Doug said. "How did that start?"

Emme smirked when Jordan groaned and edged away from her. "Do you remember that really annoying kids' song, *John Jacob Jingleheimer Schmidt*?"

"Kind of," Gilly said.

Emme propped her arms on the table. "Well, Jordan's middle name is Jacob." She tilted her head to the side. "Didn't you spend an entire year trying to convince everyone to call you J.J.?"

She looked back at Gilly. "Anyway, I got annoyed when he called me Emme Lou Who one time and changed the song to Jordan Jacob Jingleheimer Schmidt." She glared at Jordan. "And yes, it was around Christmas because that's when I started calling you Jordan Jacob Jingle Balls. I don't remember why I shortened it to Jingle Balls, though."

Jordan sighed and leaned his head back in the chair. "Because you went around singing jingle balls instead of jingle bells the entire Christmas break."

She laughed. "That's right, now I remember." Her body leaned toward Jordan, wanting to share the physical connection of their happiness, but she jerked away at the last minute. His thumb brushed across the top of her shoulder. The look in his eyes was soft and it made her want to curl into him even more. This was their last night together and they had to pretend they weren't together. Even if her parents knew, she wasn't comfortable enough with the idea of them knowing to lean against him the way she wanted.

"Are you named after your dad?" he asked.

"Kind of," her mom said.

"She was supposed to be named Emerald," her dad grumbled.

Jordan's eyebrows rose almost to his hairline and he pressed his lips together. She could tell he wanted to say something, but was holding back.

Gilly had no such problem. "Wow! How'd you manage to dodge that bullet?"

"Emmard was gone when I went into labor," Lori explained.

"Snuck it on the damn birth certificate. I called her my little Emerald for nearly six months before anyone told me the truth." Her dad had the look of a man suffering the greatest indignity of his life.

"I like Emmeline," Gilly said.

Emme winked at her. "Thanks."

"Didn't matter after a while anyway since Doug couldn't say Emmeline and everyone shortened it," her dad said.

Gilly scrunched up her face and pressed a hand against the slight swell of her belly.

"Are you doing alright?" Emme asked.

"Yeah. Little bit of indigestion. A lot of food."

"Eighteen weeks, right?"

"Right around that," Gilly said.

Emme stared at her sister-in-law's belly. She was kind of big for eighteen weeks. "Have you had an ultrasound yet?"

"We have an appointment in three weeks," Doug said.

"Have you heard the heart beat yet?"

"Not yet," Gilly said. "We've only been to see the doctor once for our initial appointment."

"Wish I had my stethoscope to see if I could find the heart-beat," Emme said.

"There's a box of your stuff up in the closet in the guest room," her mom said. "The NGO sent it when—" She swallowed hard and looked down at her wine. "Well, the NGO sent your things here."

Emme wrapped her hands around her mom's, resting on the table. She became teary eyed and her grip on Emme's hand tightened. With a tight smile, she said, "Why don't you go see if there's one in the box?"

She stood and wrapped her arms around her mom's neck, kissing the top of her head. Her mom returned her hug and patted her arm. Letting go, she jogged up the stairs and into the spare bedroom — the one she hadn't napped in — and into the small walk-in closet. She found the two moving boxes addressed to her, care of her parents, and tore the tape off the first one. The smell of old and musty clothes assailed her. Guess they hadn't washed any of her things before they boxed them up. Maybe they thought her mom would want to be able to smell her scent if she hadn't made it back. *That's a morbid thought.*

She pulled up the layers of folded scrubs, shorts, and t-shirts, but didn't find a stethoscope. The second box held all the non-clothing items — her iPod, the few pieces of jewelry she'd taken with her, some shoes, her phone, and at the bottom, three stetho-scopes. She didn't remember having three, but it was possible they had grabbed a couple from the clinic. It worked to her benefit anyway.

She dug around some more looking for her phone charger, finally it finding in a box of other cords. Plugging the phone in beside the bed, she grabbed two of the stethoscopes and went back downstairs.

Boisterous laughter, including Jordan's, greeted her at the bottom of the stairs and she smiled. Dorothy was right — there was no place like home.

She motioned to Gilly when she entered the dining room, indicating the other woman should turn in her chair. "Doug, let her lean back on you a little." Kneeling down in front of Gilly, she set the second stethoscope on the table.

"Is the other one so we can listen?" Doug asked.

"Not yet." She placed one the earpieces in her ear.

"Then what's it for?"

She gave her brother an exasperated look. "Echo location. Shh."

"Really?" His look of shock was comical. "You can do that?"

Emme rolled her eyes. "No. Now shush." She placed the diaphragm against Gilly's stomach, moving the small circle from spot to spot. It might still be too soon, but she was hoping she'd be able to find it. There! Closing her eyes, she concentrated on the small, yet distinct sound. Moving the stethoscope to the other side of Gilly's belly, she tried to find the proof of her suspicions. Maybe…right there.

Opening her eyes, she pulled the earpiece out of her left ear, setting it in the hollow behind her earlobe. Picking up the second stethoscope, she put one earpiece in and set the other one in the same spot behind her right ear. Taking both ends in her hand, she set one on each side of Gilly's belly where she had heard the heartbeats and closed her eyes.

The soft echo of two strong and steady heartbeats sounded through the stethoscopes. She smiled, opened her eyes, and met Gilly's gaze. Her eyes shone with equal parts happiness and trepidation. Emme took the earpieces out.

"Why were you listening to both sides of her belly?" Doug asked.

"Really?" Gilly asked, a little breathless.

"I'm ninety-five percent sure," Emme said.

"Oh my god." Gilly covered her mouth with her hand, her eyes wide. "I thought I was just getting really fat."

"What are you sure about? What's going on?" Doug asked.

Emme ignored him. "You need to call your doctor tomorrow and have an ultrasound as soon as you can."

Gilly nodded. "Okay." She dropped her hand. "Oh my god."

"Hello! What is going on?" Doug demanded.

She couldn't pass up the opportunity to tease her brother. "Jeez, Doug, keep up." She stood from her crouch. "You're having twins."

Her mom leapt out of her seat and jumped up and down clapping. "Twins!" Doug sat there, mouth hanging open, speechless. Her mom ran around to hug Gilly. She let her go and continued to dance around the dining room, fists raised, like she had just scored the winning Super Bowl touchdown.

Her father had his usual, bemused look on his face. "I take it Mom is excited about being a grandma," she said.

He stood and patted her back. "Don't think this is going to give you that big of a reprieve. It's probably going to make her worse."

Emme groaned. "Great."

~

Close to nine o'clock, Gilly yawned and looked down at her belly. "I guess this explains why I've been so tired." She rested her head on Emme's shoulder, where they sat on the couch, having left the men alone to talk on the back porch. "I'm glad you were the one who told us."

Emme laid her head against Gilly's. "Me, too."

Gilly raised her head, dislodging Emme. "Mostly I'm just glad you're here." Her eyes teared up and she waved a hand in front of her face. "Don't mind me. It's the hormones."

Emme laughed and bumped her shoulder against her sister-in-law's. "I'm glad, too."

Pushing up from the couch, Gilly said, "Time to go home. I need a foot rub before bed, especially now that I know I'm carrying twins."

Following her mom and Gilly through the house, they said their good-byes on the back porch. Her mom and dad walked Doug and Gilly to the front door with a parting, "Don't stay up too late."

Alone for the first time in what felt like days, rather than hours, she curled up next to Jordan on the outdoor sofa. He wrapped an arm around her shoulders and pulled her even closer.

"How close are we to the ocean?" he asked.

"Twenty minutes with traffic."

"When did your parents move here?"

"About six years ago." She stared out into the blackness of the small back yard. "There's no gazebo."

His fingers toyed with the ends of her hair where it rested on her shoulder. "A what?"

She tilted her head back to see him. "A gazebo. That's where you kissed me the first time."

He smiled. "I remember."

"I never thanked you for beating up David Baker."

"Hmm, wasn't sure you knew about that."

She quirked an eyebrow. "Kind of hard to miss the matching black eyes and broken nose he had at school the next day. He also said he was sorry for being a dick and he wouldn't do it again."

"Good to know he got the message."

"I also never had another date in high school."

He smirked. "Good."

She gasped. "How was that good? That was not good!"

"You shouldn't have been dating in high school anyway."

"I— You—" She sputtered, trying to find the words to express her outrage.

"Your dad knows we're sleeping together."

"Oh my god!" She pushed away from him. "You have to stop touching me."

"Why?"

"Because we've been together for two weeks."

"Emme, we've known each other more than half our lives."

"We hadn't seen each other for fifteen years."

"So?" His stare was assessing. "What's really going on?"

She rubbed her forehead. "I've never been comfortable 'being' with a guy in front of my parents. Even when I was married, we kept public displays of affection to a minimum." She shook her head. "I'm not even sure why, to be honest. Mom and Dad are always hugging and touching each other."

"I understand wanting to respect your parents, especially in their house. But me not touching you? That's not going to happen." He pulled her closer and locked his arms around her. "Your dad told me to call him Emmard."

She stilled. "He did?"

"Yeah. Why're you surprised by that?"

"He never let my ex call him Emmard." She deepened her voice. "'Mr. France is fine.' That's what he said the first time he tried to call him Emmard."

"Huh." He grinned. "Guess that means he likes me."

"Hmm." She mewed her mouth and rested back against his large frame, his heat seeping into her side. "Or something."

He rubbed his cheek against her head. "What time do they usually go to bed?"

"'Bout now. Mom may read for a while, but they're usually lights out by nine-thirty."

He looked at his watch. "We've got about fifteen minutes to fool around before we go upstairs."

"Oh." Disappointment settled in her chest. He had an early start in the morning, but she had envisioned their last night together differently.

His teeth nipped at her ear. "Get out of your head, Emme. I'm just giving your parents time to fall asleep."

She tilted her head back to give him more access. "Oh."

"You're going to have to be quiet."

"What do you mean?"

"You get a little loud sometimes. It's awesome since it means I'm doing something right. But I don't want your parents hearing it when I make you scream."

"Someone's awfully full of themselves."

His grin was licentious. "Someone's going to be full of me."

"Oh my—."

Jordan's mouth covered hers, his tongue sliding against her bottom lip. She inhaled sharply, desire piercing her like tiny little needles all over her body. She turned and straddled him.

"God, baby, I can feel the heat from your pussy through your shorts. Are you wet? Ready for me to slide into you? Spread you wide and fill you up?"

She gasped, his erotic words sending a gush of moisture between her legs. "Yes."

"Am I going to have to shove your face into a pillow to keep you quiet? Keep your luscious ass in air while I take you from behind?"

All she could do was pant, so close to orgasming just from his words.

"Fuck, I can't wait anymore. Let's go."

He stood and lowered her to the ground, then adjusted the front of his jeans where the bulge of his erection pressed. She licked her lips and lifted her gaze.

"Hell no," he said. "Stop looking at me like that."

She blinked. "What?"

"You're not giving me head on the back porch of your parents' house. I'm good with having sex behind a door that locks, but no way in hell are you wrapping those lips around me where either of your parents can walk in on us."

"Oh. Yeah." He was right, but she was still disappointed. "Suppose not."

He shook his head. "I like the way you think, though. Come on." Grabbing her hand, he led her back into the house, locking the door behind them.

The upstairs bath light was on to guide their way and they tiptoed to the room he had claimed earlier. Easing the door closed, he thumbed the lock with a soft click.

Emme had no time to think before she was in his arms, his hands skimming her body, touching everywhere he could reach. Her shirt was gone in moments and her pants and underwear following soon after. He left her briefly to remove his own clothes and then she was airborne as he tossed her onto the bed.

He wasted no time in planting his mouth between her legs. She drew her knees up, gripping the sides of his head, trying to pull at the short strands of his hair. God, if he ever left the Army she'd make him grow his hair out so she had something to grab while he was tonguing her clit. She inhaled sharply when sucked on it. *Like that.*

He stopped sucking. "Pillow, Emme." Finding her clit again, he flicked the tip with his tongue and glided two fingers into her core.

She bit her lip to keep from moaning, groping blindly for a pillow. Finding one, she covered her face and released a short shout. Her hips moved in time to his fingers and mouth while he fucked her, the orgasm building. Just before it crested, he stopped and grabbed her hips.

"Flip." Putting pressure on her hips, he turned her, then pulled her up on her knees. The hand in the middle of her back kept her head down and she braced her weight on her elbows.

He slid his hard cock between her slick folds. His hands left her and she heard the crumple of a condom wrapper. A moment without him and he was back, sliding his cock back and forth, wetting himself with her juices again. The tip caught her entrance before continuing on to nudge her clit, still sensitive from his mouth.

His hand reached around and found her hood. His fingers barely touched her, rubbing circles around and around.

She was so close. Just a little more pressure or if he would— His finger pressed on her clit at the same time he entered her in one smooth, hard stroke. The angle rubbed her front wall. He withdrew and slid forward setting up an alternate rhythm of pressing her clit and filling her pussy.

Heat gathered in that one spot in her core. Her thighs quivered and she buried her face in the pillow, concentrating on the feeling. So close. She just needed—

He leaned over her and nipped at the fleshy part of her shoulder.

She exploded in a burst of starlight and shoved back against him, lost to everything except the waves of pleasure coursing through her body. He stilled while she continued to rock against him, riding her orgasm through to the last little ripple.

Her whole body shook and he withdrew from her, laying her on her side and turning her. Gathering her in his arms, she felt him searching for her entrance. He slid forward again, pushing into the swollen muscles of her channel.

She took a shuddering breath, wrapping her arms around his chest. "You didn't—?"

"Not yet," he whispered.

He kissed her. Soft and gentle. His thrusts matched his kiss. He set a steady pace, rocking his hips into hers, the base of his dick pressing against her clit with every thrust. This was different. This was so much more intimate than they'd been any other time. More than just sex. More than fucking. It was romantic. He was—

She stopped the thought before it could form.

The words tumbled around in her brain, ready to be screamed from her lips, but she wouldn't put that kind of pressure on him the night before he left. More than anything, she was scared he didn't feel the same way.

The way he was… They were having sex, it felt like it, but maybe it was wishful thinking on her part.

His warm, rough hand traced down the length of her body. He hooked her leg behind the knee and drew it up around his waist. "Emme."

She found his mouth with hers, wrapped her arms around his neck and poured all her feelings into her kiss.

Please understand what I'm saying.

He continued to rock into her, picking up his pace as his breathing increased. Using his thumb, he pressed her clit and she came again, pulling both legs around his waist, clenching him tight.

The tempo of his thrusts sped up, the power of his hips driving her toward the top of the bed. She grabbed the cheeks of his ass, feeling them clench and tighten under her fingers as she rolled her hips, trying to prolong her second orgasm.

He tore his lips from her mouth and buried his face in the side of her neck, his mouth wide, breath warm and wet against her skin. He surged forward and stayed planted as his body shuddered and jerked, pouring himself into her. Grinding his hips in circles, he groaned before collapsing on her.

Tears stung the corners of her eyes as she wrapped her arms and legs around him, locking him in place. She felt him wipe his head against the pillow under her head.

"You okay?" he asked, his lips brushing against her neck.

She nodded, afraid if she spoke the tears she was holding back would burst forth.

"Am I crushing you?"

She shook her head.

"I'll move in a second, after I recover. I think you killed me," he said.

Smiling, she tucked her head into his shoulder.

Too soon, he pulled away from her. "Is there a waste basket in here or do I need to go to the hall bath?"

"There should be one by the door."

"Be right back."

Shivering at the loss of his weight and heat, she rolled to the side and pulled the sheet and blanket down, sliding between them. The bed shifted with his weight when he returned. Sliding in beside her, he pulled her to him, wrapping her in his arms. He held her so close, the fingers of his hands brushed against her ribs.

"I'm going to try not to wake you in the morning," he said.

"Jordan—"

"I don't want the last image I have of you to be crying in my rearview mirror. I want it to be you spread out in this bed, exhausted because I wore you out."

Tears pricked her eyes and leaked out the corner, but she nodded.

"And no crying now. I'm coming back Emme. It's only a few months."

"It's almost six," she argued.

"More than two, less than ten. A few." She felt his smile against her neck.

"I'm going to miss you."

"I'm going to miss you, too. But I *am* coming back, Emme. You can count on that."

"Thank you… Yes, ma'am, I look forward to meeting you in person as well… Have a good evening." Emme hit the disconnect button on her phone and grinned down at it.

She got the job. A teaching job and in Charleston, but it still put her within three hours of Fayetteville. "Woo hoo!"

Tossing the phone on the bed, she jogged down the stairs for dinner. She rounded the corner of the kitchen and kissed her mom on the cheek.

"Well, you're in a good mood. Did you talk to Jordan already?"

Snagging a dinner roll from the serving dish on the counter, she pushed down the twinge she felt every time one of them asked about Jordan. She was still weirded out that her parents knew she and Jordan were together. It'd been a month since he rescued her and they'd been apart for half of that. "No. I got off the phone with the Dean of Nursing at the Medical University of South Carolina in Charleston. She offered me a teaching position."

"Oh, sweetie, that's wonderful." She pulled the pork roast out of the oven and set it next to the beans. "Is teaching something you want to do?"

Emme shrugged. "It wasn't something I considered, but a nurse

I used to work with up in Fairfax recommended it." She took the plates down from the cabinet. "It's fairly regular hours. I'll have some clinical hours that I'll do as well, but that will depend on my teaching schedule and whether that's part of the curriculum."

"I'm very excited for you."

"What are you excited for?" Doug asked, coming in from the foyer.

"Hey! I didn't know you guys were coming for dinner. Where's Gilly?"

"Bathroom."

She nodded. "How did the ultrasound go?"

"You should probably ask Gilly. I'm pretty sure I went into a coma when both babies popped up on the screen."

Gilly rounded the corner. "He's not kidding. I had to wipe drool off his chin."

"Did you find out what they are?" her mom asked. "Boys? Girls? One of each?" She clasped the dish towel to her chest.

Gilly glanced at Doug. "At least one boy. The other baby was uncooperative and wouldn't uncross its legs."

"My money's on a girl, then," her father said as he joined them. "Uncooperative from day one." He kissed his wife on cheek, then hugged Emme with one arm. "Best thing in the world to keep you on your toes."

"Ha ha ha, Dad." Emme poked him in the ribs.

"All right you two, dinner's ready." Her mom jumped in to mediate. "Doug, help Emme finish setting the table. Gilly dear, I got you some bottled water and one of those fruit infuser bottles. I know drinking nothing but water all day gets rather dull."

Emme flashed a grin at Gilly as her mom continued to dish out advice. She grabbed the silverware and napkins and followed Doug into the dining room. They found the same routine they'd had growing up, circling the table and setting each place. "How're you really doing?"

"I kind of hope Dad's right and the other baby's a girl." He set the last plate down. "Then we'd have one of each." He ran his hands through his hair. "How long does the throwing up last?"

Emme set down the last fork and leaned her hip against the table next to him. "Conventional wisdom says morning sickness is actually a good thing and women who have it have healthier babies."

"But all day? I'm not kidding Em, she's nauseous all day long. She throws up at least twice. I asked mom to make veggie lasagna because she gags at the smell of meat. I haven't had bacon in almost three months."

"Really, Doug? Go to a restaurant if you want bacon."

He cocked his head. "You know that's not the issue."

She smiled. "I know. I just wanted to give you shit."

"I'm freaking out. I don't know what to do."

"Hold her hair back from her face. Rub her back. Get her ginger ale and saltines."

"Emme, I'm serious."

"So am I. That's what she needs from you, Doug. She just needs you to be supportive. Everything she's experiencing is normal and unless her doctor says there's a reason to worry, there's no reason to worry."

"Are you sure?"

She wrapped her arms around his waist and squeezed. "I promise Doug. I don't like you enough to lie to you to make you feel better."

He laughed, returning her hug. "You love me."

"Only because I have to."

"Glad he got you back," he whispered, rocking her side to side. "Don't think I said that before."

"Glad you went and got him," she said.

"You two quit being nice to each other," their dad said. "It's going to make me hide all the knives."

"One time, Dad," Doug said. He helped Gilly with her chair. "And it didn't even need stitches."

They passed around the serving dishes while Gilly and her mom finished discussing her appointment.

"What was so exciting when we got here?" Doug asked during a lull in the conversation.

Emme finished chewing. "Oh. I got a teaching job offer from MUSC in Charleston."

Doug, Gilly, and her father congratulated her on the job and asked when she would start. "And you'll only be an hour and a half from Jordan," her Dad said.

"Charleston is three hours from Fayetteville, Dad," Emme said.

"Yes, but he'll be in Savannah." He ate a large bite of roast, unaware of Emme's confusion.

"Why will he be in Savannah?"

"That's where his command is going to be."

Emme set her fork down. "You're not making any sense, Dad. What command?"

"The command he's getting with the promotion."

"Dad," Doug said.

She looked between her brother and father. "What promotion?"

"Dad." Doug's voice held a warning.

"I called in some favors. Got him looked at on the supplemental board."

"Dad!"

"What?"

She heard the confusion in her father's voice, not realizing he'd just dropped a bomb on her. Her lungs felt tight, as if she was trying to breathe through a wet blanket and her heart pounded in her chest.

Had he come for her because he was promised a promotion? Had he stayed to guarantee it?

Why did she feel so betrayed? It was so... So...mercenary. She knew his career was important to him — he'd said himself being the Army was all he'd ever wanted to do — but to go halfway around the world for a guaranteed promotion?

"Did he know?" she asked.

"Emme," Doug said.

"Dad. Did he know about the promotion?"

Her father shrugged. "I guess so. I know his commander told him there would be incentives to going on the mission."

Incentives. Had she been just another incentive?

"Emme." Doug's voice was earnest and she raised her gaze to his. "It's not like it sounds."

She wanted to believe that, but she needed to hear it from Jordan. "Excuse me, please." She pushed back her chair and took her plate into the kitchen.

They usually didn't video chat until later in the evening, but she'd see if he'd answer now. He had access to wifi in his room. One of the perks of being up for promotion? She shook her head. Everything he'd said and done was now in question.

What were the conditions of his promotion? Had staying in Abu Dhabi with her been one of them? She couldn't imagine sleeping with her had been one. Maybe that was just an added perk.

She closed the door to her room and logged onto her laptop. The digital ringing filled the room, seeming to echo off the walls. She was about to click the 'end call' button when his smiling face appeared.

"Hey, babe. I wasn't expecting your call for another hour. I just got done at the gym." His brows drew together. "What's wrong? Has something happened?"

Her pulse raced. What if he admitted it was all a game? "I hear congratulations are in order."

He shook his head. "Congratulations for what?"

"Your promotion and command down in Savannah."

"How did you hear about that?"

She took a shuddering breath. "Dad said one of the incentives you got for rescuing me is a promotion and command position."

He leaned back in his chair. "Shit."

Her heart shattered. He'd known.

"Emme, they told me there were incentives when they approached me, but all it took was Doug asking for my help." He leaned forward, closer to the camera.

"You're telling me you didn't know Dad set it up to guarantee your promotion?"

"I swear I never asked what the incentives were and they never told me."

God, she wanted to believe him. "But you know about it now?"

"I received the notification this morning."

"I see." She looked down at her hands, picking at the dry cuticle around her nails. "Were you going to tell me?"

"Emme, I just found out. I haven't even had time to figure out how the hell I got selected. I wasn't supposed to be up for promotion until next year."

"Was I just another incentive?"

"What the fuck?"

"Was I?"

"How can you even ask that?"

Pain tore at her. "You're not answering the question, Jordan."

"Because I can't believe you're even asking it."

"Why wouldn't I ask it? You didn't have to stay with me. Someone else could have. Was it to move up the ranks?"

"For fuck's sake, Emme. You're right. I didn't have to stay in Abu Dhabi. I could have come on this fucked up deployment as soon as you were out of Mali. I stayed because you needed me."

"How did I need you?"

"Are you kidding? You used me as an emotional crutch. I tried to do the right thing and walk away."

"Right. Because you got nothing out of us being together."

He opened his mouth to answer, but a pager beeped somewhere next to his computer. He picked it up and looked at it. "Fuck. I don't have time for this right now." He stood and she caught a glimpse of his black shorts, the same kind he'd worn in Abu Dhabi. "We'll talk in a couple of days when I get back off mission." The screen flickered black before switching to the home screen of the video chat program.

She took a shuddering breath. Would they? They'd never fought. Of course, two weeks wasn't enough time to fight about anything.

Someone knocked at her door. Mom or Dad? "Just a second." She swiped her fingers across her cheek and answered the door, surprised to find Gilly. "Hey."

"Hey. Thought you could use this." She held out a glass of white wine.

Emme pressed her lips together in a semblance of a smile and took the glass. "Thanks."

"Can I come in a sec?"

She stepped back. "Sure." She noticed the second glass in Gilly's hand. "You shouldn't be drinking. At least not right now. A glass every now and then in your third trimester won't hurt, but it still goes against doctor's orders."

"Oh, this one is for you, too. I figured the way you left dinner you were going to need two glasses."

That earned a real smile. "Thanks."

"Sure." Gilly sat in the winged-back chair beside the bed. "Did you get a hold of Jordan?"

Emme looked down at the glass and sat on the edge of the bed. "Yes."

"What did he say?"

She took a sip of the chilled wine. "That he knew there were incentives when he took the job, but not what they were."

"Do you believe him?"

Did she? "I don't know." But she did. Once she dug down deep enough in her heart, past the hurt and doubt, she knew the truth. "Yes. I believe him."

"But you're still upset?" Gilly probed.

Emme nodded and took another sip of wine.

"What bothers you most?"

She huffed. "I was wondering the same thing when you knocked on the door."

"And?"

"It hurts to think he doesn't want me for me." She looked up at Gilly. "I feel like a pawn. He didn't need to be on that mission. Titan could have rescued me fine without him and the only reason he had to go was for the promotion. It's making me question everything that came after."

"You're right, he didn't have to go," Gilly said softly. "Doug said Jordan did it because he asked him to. You still would have been rescued, but you would have been left to the care of strangers. Possibly in a hospital without your family. Your mom wanted someone you'd know to be with you and your dad moved the world for your mom. And you. I think Jordan did it for Doug."

Guilt rushed at her like a linebacker, picked up her heart, and slammed it to the ground in a blitz attack. They hadn't really talked about what'd happened to her. Her mom and dad been understandably emotional the first few days she'd been home, but they'd never discussed how everything came about. Maybe they'd been content to accept she was home and put everything in the past.

"Shit," she said. "I think I screwed up."

"How did you leave things?"

"Not good. He got paged and had to go. A mission, I think."

"But you didn't end it?"

"I don't think so?" Had she? Panic that he might think she wanted to end things made her edgy. "I don't want it to be over, but I need to know he's with me for me and not because I'm part of a package deal."

"Then tell him everything you told me and talk to him about it. When are you supposed to talk again?"

"He's said he'd call when he got back from his mission."

"Don't let your doubts get in the way of what could be the best thing in your life."

"When did you get so smart?" she asked.

Gilly grinned. "Round about twelve." She rubbed her belly and tilted her head. "I watched him with you, when he was here."

Her fear tried to wiggle its way back up into her chest. "And?"

"If I was a betting woman, I'd say you're it for him."

"I think he's it for me, too."

"I hear a *but*."

Taking a deep breath, Emme grabbed her greatest fear and shoved it out in the open. "What if it was the circumstances? Hero rescues damsel in distress and they have sex because of all the adrenaline and relief to be alive?

"Then I don't think you guys would have been video chatting every night for the past two weeks." She drummed her fingers on her belly. "Tell you what. If I'm wrong, I'll name my daughter Emerald."

Emme laughed and brushed away an errant tear. "That's a pretty bold wager. Don't think I won't hold you to that."

Gilly winked. "You won't have to."

~

*E*mme blinked awake and looked at the red digital numbers on the clock next to her bed. Four-thirteen a.m. Pulling a hand from under the pillow, she activated the touchpad on her laptop. The video chat website was still open on the screen — with no notification of a missed call.

It doesn't mean anything. You've gone longer than two days without talking to him. He could still be on a mission. The internet could be down —it's happened before. Give him a chance.

The pep talk didn't help. Every night she went to bed staring at the screen of her laptop and woke up five or six times throughout the night to check it.

An ache formed in the center of her heart. The more time went by, the bigger the ache got. Like a hole in fabric that kept getting bigger and bigger.

She sniffled and buried her head in the pillow, tears pooling under her cheek.

Please don't let it be too late.

CHAPTER 17

*H*er arms ached from being tied to the chair and her shoulder was on fire. Her cheek throbbed where her captor had hit her. "Please stop."

"You will die today, whore." Spittle hit her cheek and she flinched.

She struggled against the ropes that bound her wrists, her breathing rapid and out of control. "No."

"Allahu Akbar," his minions echoed.

No! A sob tore through her. It wasn't supposed to end like this. Where was her rescue? Where were the good guys?

She whimpered as she watched the blade rise over her head. She squeezed her eyes closed.

Pleasegod, pleasegod, pleasegod.

An explosion rocked the building, sending dust and small chunks of mud plaster raining down on them.

Emmecoughed from the dust filling the room. *Thank you, god.* She heard the *pop pop pop* of gunfire and knew he was going to come through the door and kill her captors. She just had to be patient.

The door burst open. One of the captors fell as he was shot.

Jordan strode through the door, his gun at the ready. He raised his weapon and took aim at the captor with the machete, but then he stopped.

He looked at her, lowered his gun, turned, and walked away from her.

"Jordan!" She pulled at the ropes cutting against her wrists, suddenly tied in front of her. "Jordan! Please! I'm sorry!"

The dust and smoke swallowed him as he walked away.

The machete glinted as it rose over her head and she screamed.

"Emme! Emme!"

Her father's voice yanked her from her dream and she gasped as she opened her eyes. Blinking against the bright light of her bedside table, she turned her head.

He pushed her hair away from her face. "It was a dream, baby girl."

She nodded into the pillow as a sob wracked her body. She'd had them for the past thirteen nights. Ever since she'd asked Jordan about his promotion…and he'd never called her back.

"Talk to me, Emme. You called out Jordan's name."

"I know," she whispered.

"You still haven't heard from him?"

She shook her head. He muttered under his breath and she turned to look at him over her shoulder. "What?"

"Nothing worth repeating. Do you want to tell me about your dreams?"

Shaking her head, she rolled so she was facing him. "I know why I'm having them, Dad."

"Do you?

She sighed. "I dream about when I was kidnapped, right before I was rescued. When I was—" How was she supposed to tell her dad how close she came to dying?

"I read Titan's report, Emme. I know what happened."

"Oh." That explained why he never asked about it. In a way she was grateful — she could talk about it without having to retell the events. "So you know it was close. When I opened my eyes, Jordan was standing in front of me calling me Emme Lou Who and asking if I was ready to go home." She picked at the sheet next to her hand. "In my dream he turns around and walks away. Leaves me where I am."

She chanced a peek at her dad. "You know it's just a dream, right?" he asked.

"Yes, but it still hurts when it happens. Especially since I haven't heard from him."

"Do you want me to make some calls? Track him down?"

She shook her head. "No. I can't go chasing after him like a love-sick school girl."

"You sure?"

"Yeah."

"The kind of man I think Jordan Grant is wouldn't ditch you without a reason."

"I'll try again to email him again, but it has to be his decision."

"All right. Get some rest, you've got a long drive tomorrow." He kissed her forehead and left her room, closing the door behind him.

Emme threw back the covers and grabbed her laptop from the dresser. Sitting on the edge of the bed, she checked to see if Jordan was logged onto the video chat site. No luck. He didn't believe in social media, so she couldn't even see if he had updated his status lately.

Her last option was email. Clicking on the compose button, she poured out her heart. She'd sent one every day, but this would be the last. At some point she had to admit defeat and stop running after him. She read through the email one last time and hit send.

~

ordan blinked in the dim light, trying to gain his bearings.

A hospital room. How did he get there? The back of the bed was up enough so his torso reclined a little. Glancing from one side of the room to the other, he could see he was in a single room. Judging by the low lights, it was night.

He looked around for the call button and found the control hanging from the bed rail on his right. Pain shot up his chest when he twisted. Stifling a groan, he pushed the button that looked like a stick-figure nurse. The door clicked open less than a minute later and a black man in light blue scrubs entered.

"Welcome back, Major Grant." He put some disinfectant on his hands from the wall dispenser. "I'm Captain Flores. How're you feeling?"

"Like I got hit by a truck." Jordan's tongue felt thick and dry. And fuzzy. He moved it around in his mouth trying to work up some moisture. "Where am I?"

"Fort Bragg. Womack Army Hospital. Do you remember what happened?" He logged onto the computer by the bed and began clicking away with the mouse.

Jordan struggled to remember anything that would have landed him here. The last thing he recalled was video chatting with Emme. She'd been upset about something. What was…? His promotion. She'd found out he'd been offered incentives. "I turned down a promotion."

Captain Flores's eyebrows rose and he chuckled. "Was that before or after you got hit by a truck?"

"Before, I think." He raised his head. "I really got hit by a truck?"

"From what I hear. Attempted suicide bomber tried to ram into your patrol. He got shot, but you zigged when you should have zagged."

Jordan furrowed his brows. They'd been on a mission… "I don't remember. How long ago did it happen?"

"Almost three weeks ago." He pulled a stethoscope from his pocket and put the earpieces in his ear.

"Three weeks ago?"

Captain Flores winced and pulled the stethoscope from his ear. "Not so loud, please."

Jordan dropped his head to the pillow. "Fuck. Why was I out for so long?"

"Deep breath." He listened to the lower part of Jordan's chest where he had felt the pain before removing the earpieces again. "Swelling on the brain. You were put into a medically induced coma to help you heal. I paged the doctor. She'll go over the extent of your injuries more in depth."

"Have I been here the entire time?"

"No. You spent most of the time at Landstuhl. You were flown here four days ago."

"What's up with my leg?" Jordan lifted the thin white blanket to see his leg wrapped in an ace bandage from his thigh down to mid-calf.

"The impact shattered your knee."

"Jesus." The captain went into the bathroom and returned with a large cup. "My family?"

"They're here." He handed Jordan the cup. "Well, they're in the area. They're not here right now."

"Emme?"

"Who?"

"My girlfriend. Emme France. Is she here?" He sipped the water.

The captain shook his head. "I don't recognize the name. It's only been your parents, as far as I know."

Where was Emme? Shit…did she even know? "Is there a phone I can use?"

"There is, but let's wait until you talk to the doc. Also, it's three a.m. It can probably wait a few hours."

Jordan rubbed his eyes. Maybe, but he had a bad feeling. Emme would have been here if she knew. "What time do my parents usually show up?"

"I'm not sure. My shift starts right around the time they're leaving in the evening."

Two quick knocks preceded the door opening and an older woman in a white lab coat stepped in. She looked like she should be at home in a rocking chair, knitting rather than making rounds at an Army hospital. "Good morning, Major. I'm Doctor Kelly. How are you feeling?"

"Sore." No need to repeat feeling like he got hit by a truck. "Should I still feel like this after three weeks?"

"It's not unexpected. There was extensive damage to the left side of your body." She pulled a pen light out of the breast pocket of her coat and flashed it in each of his eyes. "Pupil response is normal."

Her small fingers probed his ribs. He sucked in a breath and jerked away when she hit one spot in particular.

"Sorry." She stopped poking his side. "You fractured three of your ribs and had a collapsed lung."

He blinked. "What happened exactly?"

"You don't remember?" She moved the sheet and blanket away from his foot and pinched his toes.

"No."

Covering his feet up, she got some hand sanitizer. "Let me pull up your record." She went to the computer, clicking the mouse a few times. "The report is rather basic. You may need to talk to someone in your unit about the specifics, but it says you were hit by a small pickup truck and pinned between the front of the truck and a wall. A portion of the wall collapsed on you and caused the traumatic brain injury."

"What was the extent of my injuries?"

"The TBI, tension pneumothorax and fractured ribs, and your kneecap was shattered." She read down the list like she was reading what groceries she needed to make dinner.

"What do you mean shattered?"

"Your knee-cap and tibia were fractured and you underwent reconstructive surgery. Luckily we have a great physical therapy department. Now that you're awake, I'll put in the referral and you can begin seeing them in the next day or two."

That explained the bandage and the throb. He struggled to remember the attack, but there was a gaping hole in his memory. Not even flashes. It was as if she'd recounted something that had happened to someone else. "Is it normal to not remember?"

Her smile was gentle. "The brain is a wondrous and mysterious organ. Patients who have been through a traumatic experience will sometimes have no memory of the event. It's the brain's way of protecting itself from further harm. It could also be that the anesthesia you were given for the medically-induced coma has caused short term memory loss and you'll get it all back eventually. It's different for every person."

He pressed his lips together in a thin line and nodded. As long as he remembered Emme, it probably didn't matter that he didn't remember the attack.

"Now, I can see you wincing and trying to hide your pain, so I'm going to order some pain killers for you. They'll help you sleep as well."

"I need to make a phone call."

"And I need you to rest right now. You can call whoever it is in the morning. I'll check on you again during normal rounds." Captain Flores followed the doctor out.

Jordan blew out a breath. Damn it, he wanted to hear Emme's voice. Needed to hear it and know they were okay.

The nurse returned with a syringe on a small silver tray. He set the tray on the table next to the bed, pulled off the cap, and inserted the needle into the I.V. line. "You should begin to feel that soon."

He stared down at his arm, as if he could see the wave of warmth that was creeping up his arm. All of a sudden, his body felt weighted down, but more relaxed than he'd ever felt before. He struggled to keep his eyes open.

"Don't fight it."

"Need to call…Emme."

"You will. In the morning."

CHAPTER 18

Jordan stared at the email Emme had sent four days ago. The day after he was flown out of Germany.

I'm sorry for doubting you. If I don't hear from you, I'll know it's over.

The reply he'd sent had bounced back as undeliverable and he'd gotten a wrong number when he'd called her cell and he had no idea why it was wrong.

Panic made him restless. He wanted to punch a wall and yell. He wanted to chuck the damn tablet across the room, but then he wouldn't be able to obsess over her email. His mom, the one person who knew how to get ahold of Emme's mom, had dropped her damn phone in the toilet.

Who the fuck had he pissed off? It was like the world was conspiring against him.

Speak of the devil. The door opened and his parents entered. "Did you find it?"

"Honey, I told you I would have to look in my address book when we got home," his mom said.

"Fuck." He said in a normal voice, but he wanted to shout it at the top of his lungs.

177

"Language," his father said.

His mother stood by his bed. "Why do you need to get a hold of the France's so bad?"

He shook his head, having no idea how to explain to them everything that had happened. They didn't even know he'd gone to Mali as part of Emme's rescue mission.

The door opened again and a medical technician backed through with a wheel chair. "Afternoon, Major Grant. I'm Specialist Doyle and I'm here to take you to your physical therapy session."

"So soon?" his mom asked. "He woke up two days ago." She clutched at her hands, twisting her rings.

"Yes ma'am," SPC Doyle said. "The doctor cleared him this morning and the physical therapist had an opening."

Jordan threw back the covers and swung his good leg over the side of the bed. "Mom, I'll be fine. The doc wouldn't have cleared me if there was an issue."

"But—"

"Mom, please stop hovering."

Tears pooled in her eyes and his father wrapped an arm around her shoulder. "Jordan, you almost died. It's not unreasonable for your mother to worry."

He sighed and dropped his head. "I'm sorry, Mom. I know you mean well."

She nodded, still wringing her hands. "I don't want you to over do it and have a relapse."

Jordan took his mother's hands in his. "The doc has said I can start limited exercise. I promise not to over do it. If there's any pain or anything doesn't feel right, I'll stop. Okay?"

"All right."

He kissed her cheek. "Why don't you guys go back to the hotel. The appointment will probably be a while and I'm sure you need to pack to drive home. You can come back for dinner." He smiled. "Maybe bring me something good to eat instead of hospital food."

She gave him a small, knowing smile. "Is there anything special you want?"

Yes, he was trying to get rid of them for a while. He loved his parents, but they'd been driving him nuts for the last two days . "Nothing mashed. Or white."

"No red meat," SPC Doyle said. "I know the doc won't go for that."

His mother nodded and stepped back from the bed. His dad took her place and helped him stand. Less than a minute later, SPC Doyle wheeled him down the hall away from his parents, waiting by the elevator.

"Is it normal to be seeing the physical therapist this soon after waking up?" he asked.

"Normally you'd have started PT two or three days after surgery, but, you know."

"Coma."

"Coma."

He parked Jordan in the waiting room and grabbed a clipboard and form from the clerk at the desk. "Fill this out, best you can. I'll be back in about an hour to get you."

"Thank you."

He only got through his name and social security number before his name was called. Setting the clipboard and pen on his lap, he tried to wheel himself to the door leading back to the examination area, but knocked his extended leg into the side of the chair. The tech who had called his name wheeled him into the exam room and helped him up onto the table.

Physical therapy had better get me walking soon. He felt fucking helpless. Physically and emotionally. Damn it, he wanted to call Emme.

The door opened and Bree Marks walked in. She was wearing scrubs and her hair was wrapped in a bun on top of her head, a hospital badge clipped to the pocket of her shirt.

"Uh. What are you doing here?"

"Well." She stepped into the room and closed the door. "I'm your physical therapist." She sat on the stool and rolled close to the exam table.

"Oh. I didn't realize you worked here."

"A few years, now. If it makes you uncomfortable for me to be your PT, I'll get someone else to take your case," she said. "Your choice."

His brow pinched together. "Why would it make me uncomfortable?"

"Well, the last time we ran into each other you were a little upset."

Fuck. "The last time we ran into each other I was a head case and drunk."

"I wouldn't say 'head case.'" Her stare was level and assessing. "You sure you're okay with this?"

"Yeah, Bree. I'm good with it. Shit, should I call you Doctor Marks?"

She wheeled over to the computer and logged on. "Bree is fine. Let's pull up your file and see if they put the images of your knee in. Otherwise I'm going to have to send you down to x-ray." She clicked through the different pages until she opened up a black and white picture. "Oh yeah, that had to hurt like hell."

He tried to peer over her to see what she'd pulled up. "I don't remember it."

She looked over her shoulder. "Really?"

"Nothing."

Her head bobbled a little. "Might not be a bad thing considering the pain you would've been in." The monitor was mounted to the back wall of the desk on an extendable arm and she moved it closer to him. She pulled a pen out of her pocket and used it as a pointer on the screen. "Here. This is your patella. Looks like it split almost exactly in half. You can see where your proximal tibia fractured." She circled a portion of the x-ray.

She minimized the picture and pulled up another one,

showing bright white lines and screws. "And this is how they fixed it. There's a plate down the outside of the tibia with…six screws holding it in place and two screws in the patella."

"Fuck." He rubbed his hand back and forth across his head. "How soon until I can walk?"

"That's going to depend on how quickly you respond to treatment. Have you seen the orthopedist yet?"

"I think he's supposed to come by later today."

She walked to the door and stuck her head out, calling for someone. "Thanks. Can you page Ortho and ask them to send a consult for Major Grant? Thank you."

Closing the door, she turned to the exam table. "First things first, we need to get your muscles working again." She unwrapped thin cords from the small device she held. The cords had small alligator clips on the ends and she clipped them to large, square, foam pads. "Let's get your leg unwrapped."

He tried to help by lifting his leg, but he couldn't get the muscles to respond. It was as if his leg wasn't even attached to his body anymore.

"Relax," she said. "This is normal after knee surgery. For the next few days, the focus will be on getting your quads to respond again."

She unwound the ace bandage, revealing his swollen, discolored knee. "Is the yellow normal?"

"It's from the iodine the surgeons use to disinfect the skin." She threw the bandage in the trash. "We'll get you a new one. You've never had surgery before?" She pulled off the white gauze pads covering the incision.

Fascinated, he stared at the three-inch long line in the center of his knee. "Wisdom teeth, that's all."

"Looks good. The swelling is normal and there's no outward signs of infection. The orthopedist will give you more detailed instructions on care, but if you notice any redness or swelling around the incision or if you start running a fever, you need to let someone know."

He nodded. "What's up with the doohickey?"

She smiled and picked up the device. "This has the very original name of Electronic Muscle Stimulator, or EMS. Wanna guess what it does?"

He grinned. "Bakes a turkey?"

"Close, but no." She unpeeled the pads from the clear sheet and stuck them to his leg, two on each side, one pair close to his knee and the other farther up on his thigh. "These are going to make your quads work by sending an electrical current into your leg."

"You're going to shock me."

Laughing, she turned on the EMS. "Not enough to hurt. That's not our goal." She pushed buttons, watching his face. He stared down at his leg, feeling the brief tingling in his muscles. She pushed the button two more times and the tingle increased.

He winced and tried to pull back from the bed when pain shot down into his knee cap the next time she increased the voltage.

"Okay, back it off a couple," she said. "How's that?"

His muscle clenched, but it didn't send any pain shooting into his knee. "Good. Slightly uncomfortable."

"That's where we want it. It shouldn't hurt, but you should feel it." She set the device next to his leg. "What I need you to do is try to engage your quad when you feel the tingle. You're going to have to concentrate on contracting the muscle and it's going to feel foreign to you."

Focusing on his leg, he squinted as if that would help his muscle work. "How long do I have to do this?"

"We'll see how you're doing after fifteen minutes." She sat on the stool and wheeled over to the desk.

After a few minutes, the silence felt awkward and he searched for something to talk about. "Have you been camping again?"

"Jase and I have been a couple of times by ourselves, but I haven't gone out with a group."

"So you and he are still good?"

"Yeah."

Her voice carried the smile he couldn't see. Shit. She was a girl. Maybe she would know what he should do.

"You're a girl."

She spun on her stool, a look of amusement on her face. "Yes. Last time I checked."

"No. Yes. Fuck. I'm screwing this up." He dropped his head back in frustration and stared up at the ceiling.

"What are you trying to ask, Jordan?"

"Never mind. It's stupid."

"Whatever it is, I've been told I'm a good listener. And you don't have anything else to do for the next…" She looked at the clock on the wall. "Ten minutes."

Blowing out a breath, he told her everything that had happened from being asked to go with Titan to reading Emme's email after waking up in the hospital. "We were only together for two weeks. We've been separated more than twice that long."

"So what are you asking me? Since I'm a girl and all."

"Whether she's written me off and moved on after not hearing from me."

Bree's look was sympathetic. "The only way you're going to know that is if you ask her."

"Fuck." He covered his eyes with the heels of his hands.

"Where does she live?"

"Her family lives in Newport News, up in Virginia."

Bree cocked her head. "What about her."

He shook his head and dropped his hands. "She was looking for a new job, but last time I talked to her she was still at her parents'."

"Can you go visit her after you get released from the hospital?"

"I feel like the longer I wait the worse it's going to be. Like one of those dreams where you're running toward something, but no matter how fast your run, that thing just gets farther and farther away."

The machine beeped three times and he felt Bree's finger's on his leg. "What about this Titan company? Do they have her contact information?"

His head jerked up. "They'll have her parents' number."

She raised her eyebrows. "There you go." She ripped off one of the electro pads.

"Son of a bitch!" He slapped a hand on the now red and bald spot on his leg and glared at her.

She winked.

CHAPTER 19

*J*esus. He'd never been so nervous about anything in his entire life. Jordan stared down at the phone number he'd tapped into his phone. His finger hovered over the screen, Taking a deep breath he pressed the green circle and put the phone to his ear.

"Hello?"

"Doug?"

"Yes. Who is this?"

"It's Jordan."

"What the fuck, man. Fuck. I want to tell you to go fuck yourself and hang up, but I want to know where the fuck you've been more."

"Doug—,"

"Emme cried her eyes out for two weeks."

A knife pierced his heart. "Doug—"

"I've never seen her so unhappy."

"Doug—"

"Not even after that fuckwad in high school."

"Doug!"

"What!"

"I've been in the hospital."

"What?"

"I was injured the same night Emme found out about my promotion. I've been in the hospital for almost a month."

"Shit."

"I tried to email her, but it bounced back and I couldn't remember her cell number."

"Did you send it to the right email?" His voice was calmer, but still held an edge to it.

"I hit reply. I don't know why it wasn't delivered. Can I have her number?" He held his breath in the silence. "Please."

"I'll give it to you, but you need to go see her in person."

He picked up the pen from where it lay on the table. "Where is she?"

"Charleston."

～

*H*e'd been wrong. Now he was nervous. He wiped his sweaty palms on his jeans. Maybe he should have called instead of showing up at her office, but he hadn't wanted to give her a chance to hang up on him.

Fuck it. He stared at the closed door of the office he'd been directed to. Knuckles poised over the door, he hesitated. Maybe he should walk in. He titled his head back and forth and rapped twice.

"Come in."

Sweat beaded on his upper lip and a litany of 'fucks' ran through his head. He inhaled, exhaled, and opened the door.

Maneuvering around the door on his crutches took some effort. Stepping into the office, he scanned the small room, taking in the cubicle-style desks in the far corners, one of which was occupied by a brunette, but no Emme.

"Can I help you?"

He adjusted his balance on his good leg.. "I'm looking for Emme France."

"She's on clinical rounds."

"Will she be back in the office today?"

"No. Is there something I can help you with?"

"No. Thank you. I'll try to catch her later." Maybe he'd have better luck if he tried earlier in the day.

"Are you Jordan?"

He stopped with his hand on the knob and turned to face the woman. "Yes. Who are you?"

"Melody." She leaned back in her chair and crossed her arms over her chest. Her eyes scanned him from head to toe. "Now I understand what all the fuss was about."

He turned fully and gripped the crutches. "Excuse me?"

"I plied her with margaritas the first weekend she was here and got the whole story."

"What story was that?"

Her look was assessing. "The rescue. Abu Dhabi. Rome. Then you disappearing on her." She took in the brace on his knee and the crutches. "Although maybe you had a reason for that. What happened?"

"I think Emme deserves to hear that first."

"What's your plan?"

"Apologize. See if she still wants to make it work."

She nodded. "What do you want from her?"

"Why are you asking?"

"I'm trying to decide if I'm going to help you or not."

He stood up straight to relieve some of the pressure on his ribs. "I want Emme."

Her eyebrows raised. "That's it?"

"What else is there?"

She uncrossed her arms. "You need to make a grand gesture."

He frowned. "A what?"

"A grand gesture. You know. Sacrifice your pride and dignity and possibly make a fool of yourself."

"And what would that entail?"

Her eyes squinted and she looked like she was thinking about the best way to humiliate him. "Putting yourself out there so she has no doubt you're serious."

"As long as I don't have to run down Main Street wearing nothing but a sock and a sign."

Her lips quirked. "As fun as that might be to see, I think you'd have a hard time running anywhere at the moment." She wrote something on a sticky pad and tore off the top sheet. Holding it out to him, she said, "Get these and have them delivered to that address tomorrow. Then, show up at this classroom at exactly nine o'clock in the morning on Thursday."

"That's two days from now."

She raised her eyebrows. "You've waited this long. Thursday is the next time she has lecture and it's the best setting for what you're going to do."

"And what exactly am I going to do?"

Melody smirked. "Apologize for being an ass."

~

*E*mme checked her watch again. It was almost nine o'clock and none of her students were in the class. Pulling up the calendar on her laptop, she checked the day again. It was Thursday. She had lecture today. Jeez, she was still nervous enough about teaching. The empty classroom was freaking her out. The only reason she knew this wasn't a dream was because she wasn't naked.

She dug her phone out of her tote bag to call Melody when the doors at the top of the auditorium opened and her students filed in, one at time. Each of them held a single, long-stemmed, white rose. One-by-one, they came to the front of the class and handed her a rose, then took a seat. Each and every one wore a face splitting grin. When the last student reached her, her arms overflowed with flowers. She twisted to see four or five roses had fallen to the floor from the bundle.

"What's going on?" She stared at them in bewilderment. Several of them had their cell phones out and pointed at her.

The doors opened again and a man on crutches hobbled in. He lifted his gaze from watching his feet.

Jordan.

Taking a step back, she gasped, and clamped a hand over her mouth. Several more roses fell to the floor. He made his way deliberately down the steps, glancing up to check his progress every time he reached a wider step.

Why was he here?

Why was he on crutches?

He reached the bottom of the steps and took two long strides until he was standing right in front of her. "Hey."

"Hi," she whispered. "What are you doing here?"

"I'm making a grand gesture."

She shook her head. "A what?"

"I have it on good authority that a fuck up of this magnitude requires a grand gesture." He tilted his head behind him.

Emme looked at the top of the stairs, where Melody leaned against the wall.

"Is it too late to say I'm sorry?" he asked.

She took a shuddering breath. It'd been weeks. Months. So long ago it seemed like a dream. Something that happened in another time to another person. "Jordan—"

"I resigned my commission."

Her eyes widened. "What?"

"The day you called. I'd gotten the paperwork the night before. After talking to you and realizing what the promotion was for and what it meant, I turned it down."

"Jordan." She shook her head. "I can't be responsible for you giving up your career."

"Well, you are." He shuffled closer. "You're more important than my career. More important than anything else in my life. I'm not giving up anything. I'm gaining you."

Tears spilled down her cheek and she shook her head.

Another step closer. "I'm sorry, Emme. I would never have left you alone like that. Please give me a chance to explain."

"I have class." She gestured to the students.

"You don't," Melody said from the back. She pushed away from the wall and ambled down the stairs. "I'm covering for you today."

She knelt down and picked up the fallen roses, then took the rest of the flowers from Emme. "Go. Get sappy." Placing the flowers on the desk, she grabbed Emme's tote and held it out while pointing at the side door.

~

"Where to?" Jordan asked.

She pointed to the left. "There's a cafe down the street that serves brunch."

Even on crutches, Jordan's pace was quick enough that Emme had to fast-walk to keep up. Until he stumbled on a crack in the sidewalk and almost fell. He caught himself, but sucked in a breath and dropped one of the crutches while holding his ribs.

"Fucking hell," he gritted out between his teeth.

She picked up the crutch and helped him hop to the edge of the sidewalk. "What's wrong with your ribs?"

"I fractured a couple of them." His breathing was shallow, as if it pained him to inhale.

"How long ago?" She held out his crutch.

He leveled his stare at her. "About a month ago. The night we talked last."

"Oh." She looked at the crutches, then down at his leg. "Is that why you never called me back?"

"Yes."

"What about my email?"

"I didn't get it until a week ago. My email bounced back when I tried to reply."

That explained the email, but nothing else. "You could have called."

"I didn't remember your number. Emme." His voice held a plea and she met his gaze. His green eyes were fearful, yet hopeful. "I've been going crazy since I woke up, not being able to get a hold of you. I had to call Titan to get Doug's number. He told me where to find you." He shook his head. "I thought about calling, but I didn't want to give you a chance to hang up on me without hearing me out. I showed up at your office on Monday, but Melody said you were in the clinic. She knew who I was and she said she'd help me and she came up with this harebrained idea to throw myself at your feet and all I wanted to do was tell you I love you.

Her heart stopped then exploded in her chest, stealing her breath. Woke up from what? Why hadn't Doug said anything about talking to Jordan? He'd been here all week?

"You love me?"

"That's not how I meant to tell you." He was blushing. Jordan Grant, Army Ranger, real-life hero, was blushing.

"How did you mean to tell me?"

"Well." He reached into his pocket and pulled out a small, square box.

Her hand flew to her mouth and she stepped back, right into a couple walking past. She spun. "I'm so sorry," she told them.

In slow motion, she turned back to Jordan, still holding that box. He lifted the lid and revealed a pillow-cut, brilliant blue sapphire ring.

"I'd get down on one knee, but I've only got one at the moment."

She shook her head, overwhelmed by everything. "Jordan, it's too soon."

"It's not. You don't have to say 'yes' right now. You don't have to say 'yes' a year from now. What's important is you know I'm serious about how I feel and that I will do anything to have you in my life. I may have rescued you in Mali, but you rescued me too."

He shifted his weight. "I was going through the motions, so bogged down by all the crap that happened in the past, I couldn't see the good in the present. You showed me it was still there with your refusal to let everything that happened to you drag you down. You find beauty in the ocean and a marble roof. You make me stronger." He took a deep breath. "But I hope you say 'yes' sooner than a year from now."

She blinked back tears. "Yes."

He blinked. "Really?"

She laughed at the look of shock on his face. "Really."

Closing the distance between them, she lifted to her toes and kissed him. The crutches clattered to the ground when he wrapped his arms around her. His tongue touched her bottom lip and she opened her mouth, allowing him to swoop in.

The sound of clapping penetrated her fogging brain and she pulled away, chancing a look over her shoulder. They had attracted a small crowd, who were clapping for them.

It was her turn to blush. Setting her heels on the ground, she dropped her forehead to his chest. "My apartment is close by."

He kissed her forehead. "Lead the way."

EPILOGUE

"You're sure this is it?" Emme asked, skeptically.

"It has everything we've been looking for," Jordan said.

"Except walls."

"That's drywall. There's lots of natural light."

"Which is good since there's no electrical wiring either."

"Quit being a negative Nancy. It's a hundred yards from the beach."

Emme shrugged. "All right, I'll give you that one."

He pulled her into his arms. "This is our house, babe."

"It's a lot of work, Jordan."

"It'll give me something to do until I can start at Leonidas." He'd had to wait to be cleared by the orthopedist and physical therapist before the Army would release him. Thankfully, he'd had an in with the physical therapist and Bree had agreed to sign off on his paperwork if he agreed to continue seeing her while he was on terminal leave.

Her eyes grew wide. "You're not planning on doing all the work yourself?"

He chuckled. "Not all of it. Just the things that don't require an expert." He squeezed her hips. "You said yourself we're never going to find a house on Sullivan's Island without having to buy a fixer-upper."

"Ugh." She dropped her head back. The ceiling was peeling. She closed her eyes to block out the image and tried to picture what it would look like once it was all finished. It really was the perfect house. Five bedrooms, close to the beach, and good schools.

She raised her head and sighed. "Think it can be done in seven months?"

"I think so, but I'd have to talk to a contractor. Why seven months?"

"Because it's going to be really hard fitting a crib into my one-bedroom apartment."

"What?" He pushed her away and stared at her still flat stomach. "Really?"

She grinned. "Really."

He let out a whoop and picked her up, spinning her around. He gave her a hard, quick kiss. "You're going to marry me now, right?"

She let out an exaggerated sigh. "I suppose I should let you make an honest woman of me."

"Damn right. Want to christen our new house?"

"Um, let's wait until there isn't so much rat poop on the floor."

He laughed and kissed her again. "Rescuing you is the best thing that ever happened to me."

THE END

ACKNOWLEDGMENTS

First and foremost, thank you Cristin. I was months away from publishing my first novel when you invited me to be a part of the Titan world. *Thank you* is not enough for this opportunity.

Tara Gonzalez and Amber Addison from Ink Slinger PR and all the bloggers and readers who dive into the words and the characters and love it as much as we do.

Deidre and Kristina for your always honest and, often times, humorous comments on my initial efforts. Kristy and Toni for beta-ing (is that a word?). Jessica, for helping me plot through my block and working me into your ridiculous editing schedule. You all help me be a better writer and learn from my many, many mistakes.

To my family for your encouragement and support in everything I do.

And Team Titan - I hope I lived up to your expectations and did your boys proud.

ABOUT THE AUTHOR

Tarina has spent her entire life in and around the military – first as a dependent and then as an enlisted Air Force member.

In 2015, a friend challenged her to complete NaNoWriMo so she dusted off one of the many stories she'd started over the years, threw it in the trash, and started all over.

Tarina's debut novel, Stitched Up Heart, released in September 2016. She draws heavily from her own military experience to create authentic characters who deal with real challenges and manage to find love in the struggle.

Tarina is still active duty Air Force and a single mom of twins. Her favorite hobby is sleep. She has delusions of retiring from the military and being a stay-at-home mom and full time writer.

Follow Tarina on Facebook, FB Page, Twitter, Instagram, or sign up for her newsletter. You can contact her at tarina.deaton@tarinadeaton.com or http://tarinadeaton.com.